Savage SECRETS

VIGILANTE KINGS BOOK ONE

EVA CHANCE & HARLOW KING

CHAPTER
ONE

Madelyn

You could say it was a midnight snack that led to my broken heart.

Normally I wasn't even the late-night-snacker type. I liked sleep too much. But I'd been working for hours getting the last of my end-of-term essays written—the last essay I'd *ever* write before my final high school exams—and I still had at least another page to go. That called for some fortification.

Both Mom and my stepdad, Holand, slept like the dead, but I slipped down the stairs quietly just in case. As I opened the fridge and let the eerie artificial glow spill over me, for just a moment I flashed back to a time more than ten years ago, when I'd woken up ravenous after a bout with the flu and Dad had snuck me downstairs to make me a PB&J sandwich.

He'd probably be making me one now to get me through this essay... if he'd still been alive to do it.

I swallowed down the pang of loss that'd faded but never disappeared and reached for the fruit drawer. I'd just started to open it when the back door rattled.

With a hitch of my pulse, I straightened up and shut the fridge. The room fell into darkness. Only a thin haze of light seeped in from the streetlamps glowing beyond the kitchen window. From where I was standing, I couldn't see into the mudroom at the back of the house at all.

The deadbolt in the door clicked over. Whoever was there had a key. My mind scrambled for an explanation, knowing both my mom and Holand were upstairs. Unless one of them had ducked out without me noticing while I'd been grinding away at my essay? But why would they come in through the *back* door?

The fact that whoever it was seemed to have a legitimate means of entry was the only thing that kept me from jabbing 9-1-1 into my phone. I stood here stiffly, my hand creeping across the counter to the knife block. As careful footsteps padded inside, I curled my fingers around the handle of the chef's knife.

The cleaver was bigger, but I wasn't confident I could stab someone with that rectangular hunk of metal. Pointy seemed like a safer bet.

The basement stairs creaked faintly. I frowned. Who would sneak into our house just to go down there? The basement only held the laundry room, a storage room stacked with bins of nothing more valuable than dusty Christmas decorations, and the second bathroom.

After a moment, the hiss of running water reached my ears. Bathroom, then. My stance relaxed a little.

It couldn't be a homicidal psycho, right? A murderous lunatic wouldn't break into people's houses just to use the facilities.

And whoever it was hadn't actually broken in.

Still clutching the knife but lowering it to my side, I slunk across the kitchen, through the mudroom, and down the steps to the basement. The cooler underground air raised goosebumps on my arms, and I wished I hadn't already changed into the tank top and lounge pants I'd be sleeping in.

The sound of the water was loud enough to cover my approach. The possible intruder gave no sign that they'd realized they'd been noticed. The bathroom door stood an inch ajar, bright light spilling through the gap. Just as I walked up to it to peek inside, the person on the other side stepped right in front of that space.

He appeared so abruptly that a squeak of shock burst out of me even though I'd recognized the figure on the other side and knew he wasn't any threat. At least, not in the criminal sort of way.

The tap running water couldn't cover my yelp. Before I could retreat—if I'd wanted to retreat, which I hadn't had time to decide—the door flew open.

Logan Brooks, Holand's son and my stepbrother of three years, stood on the other side. He blinked at me, his forehead furrowing.

It was a nice forehead, broad and topped with tufts of dusky brown hair. Even nicer were those startled eyes, a lighter brown so bright they were almost gold. And that was without getting into the body beneath his chiseled face, tall and filled out with generous brawn across the chest and shoulders, tapering to a toned waist.

Okay, so Logan looked a hell of a lot more than just *nice*. He'd probably featured in the steamy daydreams of at least half the female student body at our high school. Seeing him sent a flush through all kinds of places on my own body.

"I—I'm sorry," I said, even as I realized that it was ridiculous to be apologizing for sneaking up on someone who'd just finished sneaking into a house where I lived and he no longer did. "I didn't know it was you."

Logan had moved out last summer, a month before he'd started college. He'd said he'd needed time to get settled into his new digs before classes started. But even though the college was only a two-hour drive away, this was the first time he'd come home—to what had used to be his home, for a couple of years anyway—since then. I hadn't seen him at all except for a brief appearance he'd made during the Christmas get-together with Holand's side of the family at his grandparents' house. One second he'd been grabbing a turkey leg, the next he'd vanished again.

It bothered his dad. I knew it did. Holand tried not to talk about parenting stuff with Mom around me, but

I'd noticed the dejected slant of his shoulders when one relative or another would ask what Logan was up to these days. And now the prodigal son was finally stopping by for a visit… in the middle of the night… so he could do a little washing up?

The thought of why he was here had just started to penetrate my initial surprise when Logan tipped his head toward the chef's knife at my side with a ragged chuckle. "And whoever you figured it was, you were planning on slicing and dicing them?"

I would have shot some snarky remark back, except my brain had finally caught up enough to notice the parts of him that *weren't* all that nice at all. He'd been angling himself to the side, but his head had swiveled just enough for me to notice the bruise forming at the corner of his jaw and a small splotch of red on his light blue T-shirt.

My heart lurched, and I pushed forward, dropping the knife on the little table in the hall. Logan grabbed the door to block my way, but I caught it, already having seen as he swiveled more fully toward me that there was a heck of a lot more carnage than what I'd initially spotted.

He had a scrape running across his cheekbone. A thinner cut veered from the crook of his neck down toward the back of his shoulder with blood still beading along it. And his shirt didn't just have a small splotch of what was obviously more blood. There were several larger smears and splatters across the right side, the side he'd been trying to hide from me.

He looked like someone had already been slicing and dicing him.

"What *happened* to you?" I demanded.

Logan's jaw tightened. He pushed on the door. "Don't worry about it, Madelyn. Go back to bed."

There was something a little wild in his eyes that I hadn't noticed before either. But that and the blood weren't enough to stop a prickle of anger from racing through me.

He *used* to call me Maddie. Playfully but fondly, as though we were something like friends. But, for reasons I'd never understood, that companionable familiarity had stopped sometime not long after he and Holand had moved in.

He didn't push firmly enough to stop me from coming in. He didn't want to go too hard on me— because he didn't think I could handle it, just like he didn't think I could handle whatever had brought him here tonight. I shoved past him into the bathroom before he could make a more determined attempt at shutting me out.

As I spun toward him in the small space, he caught my arm by the elbow. His eyes flashed when they met mine, and a tingle of electricity hummed through the air between us.

That had never gone away. If anything, I'd felt it more often after I'd found myself passing him in the hallway in my pajamas or sitting across the table from him at family dinners. Sometimes it seemed like he felt it too. Other times I'd thought it was all in my head.

Right now, some kind of tension was radiating off him. I could practically taste the adrenaline in the air. I had to think it was a whole lot more to do with whatever had gotten him bloodied up than with me, though.

"What do you think you're doing?" he snapped.

"I think I've been studying first aid since I was ten, and if you came here rather than going to a hospital, *someone* had better take a look at you." My gaze dropped to his shirt. Fuck, that was a lot of blood. Oh my God. My stomach lurched. "Maybe you *should* go to the hospital. If you get an infection—"

I shouldn't have said that. I knew I shouldn't have, but the situation was so crazy the words just tumbled out.

Logan cut me off with a noise that was almost a snarl and spun away from me, back toward the sink faucet that was still spewing out water. "Most of it's not mine. You think I look bad; you should see the other guy."

I stared at him, having trouble processing those words, and not just because I had the full expanse of his well-muscled back on display just inches away from me.

Logan hadn't been the type to get into fights. When he stood up to people—to jerks who deserved it—he just shut them down with his words, his confidence, and the natural intimidation that came with his size. I'd rarely seen him lay a hand on anyone.

Because I was staring at his back, I noticed a line of

red that was slowly expanding just below his shoulder blade. *Some* of the blood was his.

Logan was splashing water on his face and neck, ignoring me as if that would make me go away. I had the urge to run upstairs for the larger first aid kit we kept in the main bathroom, but I was afraid he'd take off the second I let him out of my sight. So I grabbed the smaller kit out of the cabinet under the sink, popped it open, and yanked up Logan's shirt.

I was trying to keep my mind strictly professional. It wasn't my fault that I noticed the heat of his skin and the flex of his muscles as my hand skimmed over his back.

There was absolutely nothing weird about the fact that being this close to my stepbrother got me all heated up. I'd had a crush on Logan since I was twelve, after he'd told off a bunch of junior-high bullies who'd been taunting me. That was a year before Mom and Holand had even started dating. Technically, Mom had cockblocked—pussy-blocked?—me. I should have had first dibs on the Brooks family.

Logan's head jerked around as I reached for the alcohol wipes. I caught a stutter of breath and tried not to wonder whether my touch had affected him the same way being so close to him affected me.

"What the fuck are you doing?" he growled.

"Making sure you don't end up worse off than whoever you got into it with did," I retorted. "It's going to sting. Deal with it." Then I dabbed the wipe over the narrow cut.

Logan's stance tensed with a restrained wince, but he didn't make a sound. He gripped the sides of the sink as I finished cleaning up the wound as well as I could. The bleeding seemed to be slowing—the cut didn't look that deep. But even a minor infection could be fatal given his medical history.

I smeared antiseptic cream on the spot as gently as I could manage and stuck a gauze pad overtop. The rest of his back looked unharmed, other than that cut curving over his shoulder and dipping beneath the collar of his shirt.

I frowned at it and tapped his shoulder beside the broken skin. "You're going to need to take your shirt right off for me to deal with that one properly."

"For fuck's sake." Logan whirled around to face me. His golden eyes burned into mine, and suddenly it was very hard to focus on my concern for his injuries rather than the effect his presence had on me this close up. His voice came out strained. "I can deal with the rest myself. Leave it alone."

I'd swear there was enough electricity in the room now to raise the hairs on the back of my neck with a quiver of desire. I stared right back at him, my tone firm. "You can let me help, or I'm going upstairs and telling your dad that you're bleeding all over the bathroom. It's up to you."

He glowered back at me. "Why do you always have to be so fucking stubborn, Maddie?"

The nickname gave me a giddy thrill, even though it

was the most minor of victories. "Because I need to be, obviously," I said, and tugged at his shirt.

Logan yanked it out of my hands, but he peeled it off, muttering something about how he needed to rinse it off anyway. I did my best not to ogle the expanse of his sculpted chest and focused on the cut by his neck, giving it the same treatment as the one on his back.

Logan's posture remained rigid while I worked. It was a hell of a lot harder to concentrate with him gazing down at me. The musk of his skin washed over me, mixed with a salty aquatic tang as if he'd just come out of the ocean, even though the sea was hours away.

I was more than a little giddy when I stepped back —not far, since there wasn't much space in the bathroom. The whole situation was starting to feel like some kind of hazy dream, maybe because my lack of sleep was catching up with me. Had my long-time crush-slash-stepbrother really showed up in the middle of the night all battered and bruised, or was this some weird fantasy that I'd wake up from any moment now?

There didn't seem to be any other cuts on him. The pale line of his liver transplant scar veered across his abdomen by the perfect V at the low-slung waist of his jeans, and I pulled my gaze away from it.

I'd never known Logan as anything but healthy, and he didn't like the reminders of his childhood illness. Even when he'd been living here, he'd kept the medication he still needed to take in his bedroom and gotten terse with his dad if he ever mentioned it.

"All finished," I said, a little breathless. Logan was

still tensed, his chest heaving more than I'd have expected, as if he wasn't done coming down from the fight—or was preparing for another one.

"Good," he said brusquely. "Let me finish washing up, and I'll get out of your hair."

He turned toward the small bathtub without another word, starting the water flowing from the showerhead. As he ducked just his head in to rinse off his own hair, another surge of frustration bubbled up inside me.

"And then you'll disappear for another year like we don't even exist?"

"What are you talking about?" Logan muttered, swiping the hand towel over his head and then sticking his shirt under the spray so streaks of blood coiled through the water spiraling down the drain. "I just saw my dad a few weeks ago."

"Right," I said. "You saw your dad for a coffee or something. You haven't come back *here* since you moved out. We were kind of family for a little while, in case you don't remember. Actually, you obviously do, or you wouldn't have thought you could just drop in and use our bathroom."

"I was halfway through high school when Dad and your mom got married. It was a little late to start picking up new family members. Shouldn't you be getting to bed?"

The words hit me like a slap. Which was probably why I spat out the last thing I'd have wanted to admit to him if I'd been thinking straight. "Did it ever occur to you that maybe *I've* missed *you*, you jerk?"

The complaint might not have been totally fair—or maybe it was way too accurate. The fact was that I'd been missing the Logan I'd fallen for back in junior high since way before he'd moved out. From the moment he'd started distancing himself from me, leaving rooms as I entered them, not meeting my eyes during those random encounters passing in the hall...

He looked back at me now with a jerk of his head as if the question had startled him. His mouth twisted. "Maddie..."

Before he could figure out what he was going to say, I noticed the bandage I'd done my best to fix to the curve of his shoulder was coming detached. With a curse under my breath, I leapt forward to stick it back down. But Logan's efforts with the shower had left the tiled floor slick from errant spray. My socked feet slipped, and I careened over the edge of the bathtub.

The shower water splattered my hair and tank top. Logan caught me an instant before I banged into the opposite wall and yanked me upright. He spun me away from the tub, glaring down at me—and then something else flickered in his expression.

I was abruptly aware of how the wet tank top clung to my skin, particularly the curves of my breasts. I wasn't wearing a bra. My nipples stood out against the drenched fabric, and I'd swear they tingled to sharper attention as Logan's gaze raked over them.

His hands tightened where he was gripping my

upper arms. He closed his eyes, and a tremor passed through his body. "I'm trying to do the right thing here."

I didn't know what he was talking about. It was hard to focus on anything except his touch and the way my body was screaming for him to press even closer. I couldn't stop myself from resting my hand on his chest. My voice tumbled out of me with an unusually husky quality. "So am I."

"*Fuck*," Logan rasped, and the next thing I knew, he was tugging up my chin so his mouth could slam into mine.

The kiss was hot and feral, and it short-circuited my brain. I didn't know how to do anything except kiss him back with all I had in me. His chest grazed mine, sending sparks through my nipples.

Logan groaned at the contact, the sound reverberating into me, and some part of me decided that this was definitely a dream. But it was a fucking fantastic one, so I'd better milk it for all it was worth.

More sparks leapt across my skin everywhere Logan touched. He swept his hands down my sides to my thighs, pausing to massage my ass while his tongue invaded my mouth with searing passion. Then he hefted me onto the edge of the sink without breaking the kiss.

My legs splayed around his hips. He was all over me, his mouth branding mine, his chest scorching, an undeniable bulge behind the fly of his jeans rubbing against my core.

A heady shudder raced through me, and my pussy

clenched even as it soaked my panties. I groped at Logan, trying to somehow pull him even closer. My teeth nicked his lip, but he just kissed me harder with another groan.

His hands came up to yank up my damp top, with a strangled sound of approval as he cupped my bare breasts. I gasped against his lips at the jolt of bliss he summoned with one swivel of his palms. Clutching at his neck, I barely remembered to be careful of the bandaged spot. My back arched, pressing my pussy against his groin, and Logan's breath stuttered.

In one smooth movement, he yanked my lounge pants and panties down together without displacing me from the sink. His hand dipped between my legs and found the slickness pooled there.

"Oh, God," he muttered.

A whimper spilled out of me at the contact. God was right, because I was definitely in some kind of heaven.

I fumbled with the door of the medicine cabinet over the toilet and managed to wrench it open to grab the box of condoms stashed there. I made a point of never thinking about why exactly our parents would want to have protection available on every level of the house.

Logan snatched the box from me without a word and retrieved a packet even as he unzipped his jeans with his other hand. His mouth crashed down on mine. His lips and tongue continued their savagely divine assault as he prepared himself.

He rubbed the head of his cock over my pussy from clit to slit, and I practically came just like that. But then he paused, his mouth pulling away just an inch. He was panting, his voice even rougher than before in its plea. "Tell me you're not a virgin."

I sputtered a laugh. "Of course not."

Logan drew even farther back, his eyes abruptly darkening. "That fucker Scott Camden?"

I scowled back at him, momentarily distracted from the deliciousness of this dream. "I did date him for almost a year. I'm not a nun." Logan had always seemed irritated by Scott, though he'd never made any concrete complaints. And him getting pissed off about it now was particularly ridiculous considering— "How many girls did *you* give it up to on the first fucking date?"

Logan dropped his glower, looking briefly abashed, which confirmed enough casual hookups to send irritation flaring through *me*. But then he leaned close again, his forehead coming to rest against mine, and said in a voice so taut it tugged at my heart, "None of them were you."

I wasn't sure what to make of that either, but I did know I wanted to get this moment back on track before he had another change of heart. I gripped the side of his face and said, "It's me now." Then I yanked his mouth back to mine.

He growled against my lips, grasping my thigh, and plunged into me. He filled me so fast and well that a gasp jolted out of me.

With only a few pumps, he found just the right

rhythm to send me soaring higher, faster than I'd ever thought was possible. With every roll of his hips, he drove the memory of those mildly satisfying hook-ups with my ex farther from my mind. I raked my fingers over the wet strands of his short-cropped hair, swaying to meet him as well as I could in my precarious position.

Logan kept his hand on my thigh to steady me and teased the other down my spine. His mouth traveled from my lips along my jaw and down the side of my neck, blazing a path over my skin. When I moaned, his breath stuttered.

"So fucking good," I thought I heard him mumble. "Even better than I imagined."

The possibility that he'd already imagined us doing this set me even more aflame. I trailed my fingers down his back, groped the solid planes of his ass, and moaned again when he thrust even deeper inside me.

He braced his arm against my back to curve me over and sucked the tip of my breast into his mouth. At the same time, he tucked his other hand between us. He flicked his tongue over my nipple as he pulsed his thumb against my clit and rammed into my pussy again.

I shattered. A cry that was almost a sob burst out of my throat. My head tipped back against the mirror, pleasure washing over me and wringing me out.

As the afterglow rippled through me, Logan pounded into me a few more times before following me over with one last groan. He eased to a stop, raising his head to lean it next to mine, still holding me in place on the sink. His heat wrapped around me.

I clung on to him in a daze. What happened now? Did I wake up?

Logan withdrew slowly and carefully. His jaw worked for a second. His expression had gone totally opaque, but his chest was still heaving as he recovered his breath.

He zipped up his jeans and eased me off the sink like I was a porcelain figure he was afraid of dropping, pulling my tank top back down over my chest. I reached to retrieve my pants and shimmied into them, still uncertain about where we stood.

"Thank you," he said in a tight voice. "For looking after me. I'm okay. You should really get some sleep." His tone lightened just slightly. "I don't want to be responsible for ruining your perfect attendance record."

There was enough of teasing note in that last line for me to relax a little. I touched his arm, thinking of the blood, the scrapes and cuts, the explanation he'd never really given for them. "Are you sure—"

"I'm fine, Maddie," he said firmly. "It was just—a thing. No big deal, really. I was a lot closer to the house than to my apartment, so I thought it was better to get cleaned up here. That's all. It's over."

That wasn't enough of an answer, but I didn't want to ruin whatever connection we'd just formed by badgering him more. "Okay," I said, holding his gaze.

He looked back at me and gave me a crooked smile.

I thought we came to some sort of silent agreement. I thought this was the start of something different.

So I caught his hand to give it a quick squeeze and headed back upstairs, thrilled by the thought that the boy I'd loved for a third of my life wanted me too, still half expecting to wake up and find out I'd dreamed the whole thing.

But I was wrong about a couple of things. I hadn't dreamed it. And nothing was different at all.

After those last words in the basement bathroom, I didn't hear a peep from Logan Brooks for two long years.

CHAPTER
TWO

Two years later

Madelyn

"It's not like one night of actual fun will kill you," Keeley teased as she leaned closer to the mirror propped on her dresser. She drew her eyeliner in a fine, winged line that I knew I'd never be able to replicate on myself. Which was fine. Makeup was my roommate's thing and not so much mine, which was part of the reason she was teasing me.

I rolled my eyes playfully, throwing my cozy hoodie on over my tee and jeans, which was more about warmth than anything resembling dressing up. Even though it was technically spring now, the chill in the early April air could still be biting, especially after the sun went down.

"*I* think hearing about recent medical developments is fun," I reminded her. "The guy doing the talk is one of the top researchers at this cutting-edge facility in France. This is the first time he's come to the US—I'm lucky he's giving a presentation only an hour's drive from here."

Keeley tsked her tongue. "Or you could come to the club with me and my friends, and we'd see about getting you *really* lucky."

I laughed. "Hey, maybe I'll pick up some hot science geek at the lecture and bring him back to the dorm with me. Watch out for a warning note on the door."

Keeley glanced over at me as if evaluating whether I really had it in me to do something like that. "I'd be more than happy to crash elsewhere. You work, like, twenty-five hours a day, eight days a week. Everyone deserves a break. And hot dudes. Especially on a Friday night."

I shot her a warm smile. "Maybe next week."

My roommate let out a skeptical hum, but she didn't heckle me any further. Right now, she might have been giving the impression of a ditzy party girl more concerned about having a good time than passing her classes, but her double major in political science and psychology and the honors GPA she maintained told a different story. We just cut loose in different ways.

She swept her tight black curls back from her dark

face and fixed it into a super cute updo. With a swipe of lipstick across her mouth, she straightened up and grinned at me. "Well, let's both kill it, then."

I poked her in her shoulder, taking in her shimmery club dress. "I think you'll be doing most of the killing, but that's okay."

"We really would love for you to come along with us sometime, you know," Keeley said as we headed out of the room and down the residence's staircase together. "I'm not just saying that. It's a good time. We hang out at my bestie Carmen's place for a couple of hours just chilling, and then we hit the dance floor. I know there's a wild girl under that carefully controlled exterior somewhere, just waiting to burst out."

"I promise you'll be the first to meet her."

We emerged at the edge of the parking lot. It was only late afternoon, giving me plenty of time to drive over to the conference center that was hosting the talk and grab a quick bite to eat before the seven o'clock start, but the breeze was already nippy. I zipped up my hoodie, my gaze skimming over the lengthening shadows stretching from beneath the rows of cars.

A cluster of passing students distracted me. I found myself checking each face before I jerked my eyes away, reining in my automatic curiosity. None of them had been the guy I was looking for anyway.

I'd transferred to the same university as Logan three months ago at the start of the winter semester, and our paths hadn't crossed yet. I didn't know if he even realized I'd made the transfer from my original college in our hometown. I hadn't wanted to ask around about him, which would make me feel even more stalker-y than I already did.

I hadn't *actually* stalked my stepbrother here. I'd wanted to attend the Life Sciences program at this university since before anything had happened between us. It wasn't like I'd expected anything from him anyway. He'd made it clear that he wanted nothing more to do with me when he'd blocked me all over social media as well as by phone the day after our hookup and shut me completely out of his life.

My skin tightened at the thought of the brutal rejection. It still stung a little, sure. And every time I heard a deep chuckle or saw a tall, well-built form at a distance, my pulse might have jumped before I determined it wasn't him. But the healthiest thing for me to do was to erase him from my mind as utterly as he'd erased me from his life. Apparently not just our hookup but the years of casual friendship before our parents had gotten married meant nothing to him, so why should they matter to me?

I strode along the middle row of cars as if I could outrun those thoughts. I always parked my Chevy in the same area, right over...

I stopped several cars from the end of the row, staring at those ahead of me and then sweeping my gaze back in the other direction. My mouth tensed with a frown.

I could have sworn I'd parked in this row after my last trip off campus. I'd been in such a hurry this morning that I couldn't remember if I'd noticed the car then, but I knew I'd seen the familiar green hood with its dented bumper just yesterday evening when I'd walked by on my way back from grabbing dinner.

Keeley had stopped when I had, flipping her keys in her hand. "Is something the matter?"

"My car isn't here," I muttered, confusion starting to give way to a quiver of panic. I scanned the other rows and spun around to march back the way I'd come—and jerked to a halt by an empty stall right around where I thought I'd parked.

This *was* the place where I'd left it. Last week I'd driven down a muddy lane that'd left a red clay-like dirt all over the undercarriage. It'd been flaking off in bits and pieces, and I could see a few fresh chunks of it on the asphalt now, undisturbed by yesterday's rain. The car *had* been here last night, and now it wasn't.

"What the hell!" I blurted out. "Someone stole it."

And not just my car, which I'd bought with my own savings. The flicker of panic turned into a wash of cold horror. I hadn't kept much in the vehicle, just things like lip gloss and mints and an emergency blanket in the trunk, basic objects that could be easily replaced. But there'd also been Dad's trinket box.

That wasn't anything fancy either, but the simple black lacquer box with its silver Celtic knot on the lid couldn't be replaced specifically *because* it'd been Dad's. He'd always kept it on his desk—every time I saw it, it reminded me of our long talks when he'd listen to me babble on about my childish scientific ideas and guided me with his own knowledge.

Having it with me kept his memory close even hours from home here at college. I'd kept it in my glove compartment with my insurance documents inside. If the car was gone, I'd lost that piece of Dad too.

"Seriously?" Keeley said, knitting her brow. "Are you sure you didn't just park it somewhere different?"

"Completely. That mud came off it." I pointed to the reddish bits in the empty spot. "And it's not anywhere else in the lot. I couldn't have parked in a totally different area of campus without realizing it, right?"

My voice had started to get squeaky. I inhaled deeply to try to calm myself down. Freaking out wasn't going to solve anything.

Keeley swore under her breath. "This is getting ridiculous. I've heard of a few other people who've had their cars stolen off campus parking lots in the past couple of months. Whoever these pricks are, they're— well, they're *major* pricks."

It wasn't just me. Then maybe—

"Did the other people get their cars back?" I asked.

She bit her lip. "Honestly, I'm not sure. I only heard about the thefts, not anything getting resolved. The campus police can be kind of useless for anything where there isn't, like, video evidence."

"Video." My gaze shot to the security camera perched on a post at the edge of the lot, but the frayed wires poking from its base told me it still hadn't been replaced. I let out a groan.

"I could go to the regular police," I suggested.

"They'll just toss it back to Camp-Po. I don't know how much effort those guys will put into tracking down a car for someone whose parents aren't pouring money into the school. But it's worth a shot." Keeley paused and snapped her fingers. "Or you could try talking to the Vigil."

"The Vigil?" I said. The term sounded vaguely familiar, as if I'd heard it mentioned in passing, but I'd never paid enough attention to determine what it was.

Keeley nodded eagerly. "Yeah! They're kind of awesome—from what people say, anyway. It's this group of guys that've set themselves up like PIs on campus. At first, everyone thought they were a joke, but they've solved a bunch of issues. Everyone says if you have something stolen or someone sabotages your work or anything like that, they can usually sort it out."

"Really?" The whole situation sounded a bit weird to me. "Are you sure they could handle something as major as a stolen car?"

"I don't know for sure. This girl in one of my seminars said they tracked down her phone when it got snatched. It couldn't hurt to try, right?"

The tendrils of fear gripping me eased back a little now that I had a tentative plan. "I guess it couldn't. How do I find these guys?"

Keeley waved to the east. "They've got a sort of office in the back of the law library. They hang out there a lot during the day when they don't have class—it might not be too late to catch them now. Or if they're not in, the librarian could have contact info for them."

The longer I dawdled, the more chance I wouldn't be able to catch them until after the weekend. Who knew where my car would have ended up by then? If I couldn't find them, then I'd see if Camp-Po would prove themselves more useful than Keeley had said. But it did make a little sense that students who knew the inner workings of the school on that level might be able to trace the path of a crime and pick up clues faster than the people who just oversaw campus from a professional distance.

"Okay, I'll give it a shot," I said. "Thanks!"

"I hope they can sort it out—and fast." Keeley glanced toward her own car and hesitated. "Do you want me to come with for moral support or whatever?"

It was really sweet of her to offer, especially when she had plans and it wasn't like we were super close. I gave her a smile I hoped was reassuring. "Don't worry about it. You've got dancing to do and hot guys to snag. I can manage a walk across campus."

"Well, good luck!"

I raised my hand in farewell and hurried off along the campus paths toward the law library, which I had a vague impression lay a few buildings over, in the bottom of the Business Studies building. The brisk pace started to smooth out my jangling nerves. I became more aware of the chill outside as the breeze tugged at my long, pale hair. With a shiver, I pulled my hood up.

Thankfully, the campus was better with signage than security technology. After just a minute, I spotted a signpost that confirmed I was heading in the right direction. As the stone building loomed up ahead, my pulse sped up again.

It was no big deal. I'd go in, plead my case, and see what happened. Hell, these Vigil guys might not even be there.

I pushed past the doors into a vast, quiet room nearly as big as the first floor of the main library. At the front of the room, a checkout counter stood across from a few rows of study tables. A dozen or so long shelving units stuffed with books formed aisles along the back half of the space.

No one stood behind the counter. Was I too late to even talk to a librarian? I hustled past the tables and caught a rustling sound from farther down the aisles of shelving units.

A girl who didn't look more than a couple of years older than me was standing in the third aisle with a cart of books, tucking one into its place on the shelf. She had an official-looking tag on her cardigan, so I guessed she was one of the student workers.

She glanced over when I appeared at the end of the aisle. I must have looked a little panicked still, because her face immediately turned serious with concern. "Can I help you with something?"

"Um, yeah," I said, plastering on my best smile. "I'm looking for the Vigil's office? Someone told me—"

She let out a light laugh and nodded. "Yeah, that's

here." She gestured to the wall behind me. "It's the last door toward the back of the library, past all the study rooms. I think the guys are in."

Her gaze lingered on me with obvious curiosity as I mumbled my thanks and hurried in the direction she'd indicated.

Doors did line the wall on that side of the space. Most of them had rectangular windows that allowed a view into the study rooms with their plain tables and chairs, but the one on the end offered no view inside. The wooden door held no sign. There was nothing to confirm anyone was inside or even what it was used for.

But the library assistant had sounded totally confident. I squared my shoulders and raised my fist to rap my knuckles against the door.

A friendly male voice filtered through the wood. "It's open!"

Well, that guy sounded like a helpful type, at least. Slightly reassured, I grasped the handle and pulled the door wide.

There were three figures in the room on the other side, but my eyes caught on the one closest to me, who was standing just a few feet from the doorway and turning to see who'd come in. As our gazes collided, my breath snagged in my throat.

I was staring at Logan Brooks.

CHAPTER
THREE

Madelyn

I couldn't peel my eyes away from Logan's face. All the tightly suppressed emotions I'd worked so hard to avoid rushed to the surface with a vengeance. My hands had clenched at my sides, my heart thumping twice as fast as before, bracing warily against whatever move my stepbrother might make next.

But it wasn't just alarm clanging through my body. No, there was even more anger than I'd known I was holding in. At him over the way he'd ditched me, at my bad luck that I'd come face to face with him with zero preparation.

Logan's brawny body had gone as rigid as mine. He stared back at me, his mouth forming a flat line, his golden eyes turned hard as steel. Oh, he wasn't happy to see me either? Well, he'd just have to deal with it.

I managed to wrench my gaze away to take in the

rest of the room—and the two other guys who were witnessing our stare-down. The moment I caught sight of them, everything made a little more sense.

The guy perched on the edge of the small room's central table was Slade Galvezo, Logan's best friend. When I caught his eye, he grinned with a flash of his even teeth. His wavy, dark brown locks tumbled a little farther below his ears than they had in high school, and his body filled out his button-up and jeans to more impressive effect than I remembered.

I'd seen him in the halls of our high school, he'd still looked like a boy. Now he was all man. But his playful dark brown eyes and bronze skin remained the same.

He gave me a beckoning wave, hopping down from the table. "Come on in. You don't need to be shy."

He landed with perfect balance, but his pantleg shifted on the descent, drawing my gaze to his bright red sneakers—and the vibrant blue prosthetic that briefly showed above one.

Slade could handle himself on his feet so easily you'd never know it was there, but he'd never made any effort to conceal the prosthetic, often getting a kick out of telling other students stories about how he'd lost the bottom half of his leg. I seemed to recall "hacked off by a woodchipper," "chopped in two by an ax murderer," and "eaten by a tiger when I fell into the enclosure at the zoo" being among the assortment. I had no idea what the true story was.

At Slade's beckons, I moved forward automatically, and Logan backed up just enough to let me in. Stepping through the doorway, I glanced away toward the other major pieces of furniture in the room: a long, narrow desk with a computer on it, with a matching wooden filing cabinet next to it. The third guy was sitting at that desk, peering at me much more pensively than Slade had, though his eerily bright green eyes flicked up and to the side every second or two rather than holding my gaze.

That was how Dexter Wright, Logan's other closest high school friend, had been for all of the few years I'd known him. Eye contact was not his forte. *He* still looked almost exactly like the awkward, slightly gawky boy he'd been when he graduated high school, his curly black hair a jumble atop his pale, narrow face, although the lines of his features had sharpened with maturity.

A few more chairs were strewn haphazardly around the cramped room, and closed file folders scattered the table behind Slade. Books were piled seemingly at random on the small bookcase across from the desk. A corkboard hung on the back wall, the only thing in the space that was free from clutter... because there was nothing currently pinned to it.

Easing to the side so I wasn't facing Logan quite so directly, I pulled down my hood. Slade blinked and then chuckled. "Madelyn! Long time no see."

He must not have recognized me before with my face shadowed by the hood. We'd never exactly been close, since he was a year ahead of me and my close friend circle hadn't overlapped much with Logan's.

Even though his laugh had been warm, I had the

impression that he'd flinched a smidge away from me before settling back into his casual pose. That was weird. Had Logan told him something about me—something off-putting?

My head jerked back around so I could focus on my stepbrother again. Logan was watching me. His stance had relaxed a little, but his eyes were still hard and guarded.

"What are you doing here, Madelyn?" he asked curtly.

I gritted my teeth at his tone. Part of me wanted to launch into a tirade about how he'd treated me for the past two years, but I didn't really want to air our dirty laundry in front of his friends if they didn't already know. Anyway, I'd come here for a different reason, and that problem hadn't gone away just because I'd been reminded of a different one.

"This is where people come to get help with crimes on campus, right?" I said. "You're the guys who call yourself 'the Vigil'?"

"You obviously already know that, or you wouldn't have come looking," Logan replied with a thread of snark in his tone. He spoke slowly, almost patronizingly, and my jaw clenched tighter. If he was trying to make me feel as unwelcome as possible, he was doing a bang-up job of it.

It wasn't really surprising that these guys were playing detective around campus, now that I'd gotten over my initial shock. Logan had at least used to be something of a crusader, and he and his friends had been at the center of a lot of the social activity at our high school. He knew how to make connections. And he'd always liked seeking out a challenge.

I willed my own voice to stay even. "Well, good. I just found out that my car's been stolen off one of the residence lots. My roommate said the Vigil might be able to help track it down."

Logan raised his eyebrows in a way that made me want to slam my fist down his throat, and I wasn't normally a particularly aggressive person. "Did you park it somewhere new, maybe?" he asked, all nonchalance now. "It could be you just misplaced it."

I would not scream. I would not yell in his face. I would be a picture of total calm in the face of his extreme jerkishness.

"No, Logan, I didn't *misplace* my car," I said. "I always park it in the same lot, and it's not there at all, and I can see exactly where it *was* before some prick stole it."

He shrugged. "Well, we've got a lot on our plates right now. You should find out what the police can do for you."

Slade's head twitched toward Logan at that comment as if it'd startled him. Dexter's brow knit for a second. Turning down people was *not* what made these guys so popular around the campus, and Logan was just going to send me away, knowing that I'd probably never receive justice without their help?

Dexter must have felt the need to support his friend, no matter what he thought of his answer. He spoke up, his voice quiet. "The city police are occasionally on the ball. It's worth trying them."

That statement wasn't any more reassuring than Logan's dismissal had been. Slade stayed silent, though. Clearly Logan still ruled the roost here, and his friends would fall in line.

And here he was, when I actually needed him for something not at all personal, something he'd done for who knew how many other people, and he was still pushing me away.

My frustration overflowed. "Are you kidding me?" I snapped at Logan, sharply enough that his eyes widened. "You'll help out strangers all across campus, but you'll turn away your own stepsister?"

I should have expected him to meet my frustration with his own snark. Logan wasn't the type to take blows in stride.

"I help people who need to be helped," he shot back. "Your mom's got enough money to buy you a new car without batting an eyelash, so it's hardly a big deal, is it?"

I glowered at him. "My mom works hard, but she's not *rich*, as you should know, considering you lived in her house. And I wouldn't ask her for the money she worked hard to earn anyway, not when it'd mean she couldn't do things she deserves for herself."

"Then that's your choice. You're a capable woman, aren't you? You can survive without a car."

I didn't want to admit the other aspect of the situation. Just thinking about what else I'd lost brought a burn into the back of my eyes, and showing distress in front of Logan would be *way* worse than snapping at him.

But he was stepping toward me as if to usher me out of the office, and nothing else I'd said had made a difference. It was the last card I could play. Even if he'd probably call it stupid and send me packing just the same.

I had to try. For Dad.

"It's not just the car," I said, my voice strained. "I had something that belonged to my dad in the glove compartment. I can't just buy a replacement for that."

I'd braced myself again for whatever cutting response I'd get. Instead, Logan froze. Dexter leaned forward, his gaze fixing on me for a few seconds this time before darting away, as if the admission had interested him too. Slade rubbed his jaw with a casual cock of his head, but something about his reaction niggled at me too.

Why would anything to do with my dad matter to those two, who'd never even talked to me about him the way Logan had? I wasn't sure they even knew my dad was dead and not just divorced from my mom. Of course, Logan could have mentioned it at some point.

Some of the hostility had faded from Logan's expression and voice. Now he was only grimly serious. "Something that belonged to your dad? What, exactly?"

"A black lacquer trinket box," I said, showing the size of it, about eight inches long and half as wide, with my hands. "He used to keep it on his desk. I stored my insurance papers and stuff in it. It's not worth much to anyone but me, but it's the only thing of his that I brought with me to campus."

Logan nodded slowly, and a tentative sense of relief tickled through me. He might not have been willing to give me the time of day over my stolen car, but he understood how much the loss of a parent hurt. His mom had died when he was just a couple of years older than I'd been when Dad had passed.

He hadn't really wanted to help me, though. For a second, I considered just walking away rather than having to spend another second in his presence. Did I really want to put myself through that potential agony?

But the thought of the box and of the boy I'd once considered a friend held me in place.

Maybe if we worked together on this case, I'd have the chance to figure out what the hell was up with him. Anyway, whether he liked it or not, he owed me for all the crap he'd put me through. I wasn't letting him off the hook, not when something this important to me was at stake.

When he didn't say anything, my momentary relief drained away. I folded my arms over my chest. "So, are you going to work your Vigil magic or what? If you've got some other objection, let's hear it."

His lips curved into the slightest smirk. "Someone's feisty today."

"I just want an answer. I'm not going to beg you."

"No? Not even for this oh-so-special box?"

Was he just needling me every way he could?

Suddenly I felt exhausted. I wasn't going to plead, and it was starting to seem like he intended to do nothing more than drag out this encounter as long as he could to punish me for daring to ask, only to kick me aside yet again. Maybe Camp-Po or the city police department would be good enough after all.

"Fine," I said, annoyed by the roughness that'd crept into my voice. "Obviously you don't give a shit, so I'll just go."

I turned my back to the guys and reached for the door. As my fingers closed around the doorknob, Logan's voice rang out, taut with reluctance but determined all the same.

"Wait. We'll take the case. We'll find your car."

CHAPTER
FOUR

Madelyn

Evening was falling by the time we made it back to the parking lot next to my dorm building. I wasn't sure Logan and his friends would be able to turn up much evidence with the sunlight fading, but they'd seemed determined to get started right away.

I marched straight to the still-empty spot where my car had once been and pointed. "That's where I parked."

The guys stalked over. Dexter walked right to the edge of the stall and pulled out his phone, while Logan and Slade came to a stop next to me. Logan looked at me rather than the parking spot.

"When did you see the car here last?" he asked, all briskly business, no emotion in his tone.

"Last night," I said confidently. "I was coming back from the dining hall, and I remember glancing over and thinking about how I was going to take the drive I meant to tonight. I had a lab for my first class this morning, and I was distracted planning for that when I headed over, so I wasn't paying attention then. And when I came back to the dorm in the afternoon, I went in a different door where I couldn't have seen it anyway."

Logan nodded and turned toward Slade, effectively shutting me out of the conversation. "We're looking at about a twenty-four-hour timeframe then," he said. "During most of those hours, there are students in and out of this parking lot regularly, so it'd be difficult to get away with breaking into a car and stealing it."

"The security camera's broken too," Dexter pointed out without even looking up. He must have noticed while he'd been walking over. He snapped a couple of pictures of the empty spot with his phone and then crouched down closer to the asphalt.

"Another victory for campus security," Slade said with obvious sarcasm. He shook his head, shifting his weight from his prosthetic leg to his other leg. "Well, it doesn't take a genius to convince students that the thief locked his keys in his car or something. Anyone with decent social skills could convince bystanders that there's not a crime being committed. I've done it plenty of times."

My attention shot toward him, and Slade only gave me a wink as he pulled a small candy from his pocket and popped it into his mouth. Was he kidding me, or was that the truth? I suddenly found it easy to imagine him conning his way into a flashy sports car to zoom around town. But I hadn't thought he was quite that casual about things like the law.

"That's… good to know," I said.

Logan glanced over his shoulder at me. "Did you lock the doors to your car, Madelyn?"

Both the question and the authoritative way he said my name irked me. I rolled my eyes. "Of course I did."

"And you definitely didn't leave the key someplace a thief could grab it?"

I grimaced and fished the key out of my pocket. "It's right here. I'm not an idiot. Do you always blame people when their property is stolen, or is that a privilege you save for me?"

He shrugged, letting the question roll right off him. "We have to cover every possibility." He focused on Slade again, giving me his back. Disregarding me so easily after his stupid questions. "With a new-ish car, chances are they managed to clone the key fob at some point, so it wouldn't have been an obvious break-in. But they couldn't have known whether someone walking by would know the car is Madelyn's. I don't think it's likely that the thief would have wanted to risk that. It'd be a lot easier to conduct a major theft under the cover of darkness."

"The three other cars that've been taken in the last couple of months went missing overnight too," Dexter put in, calmly analytical. He bent forward, still studying the ground. "There's some bits of red clay-like dirt here. I don't think that would have come from anywhere on campus."

"That's from me," I said quickly, impressed that he'd realized it was significant. Clearly his observational abilities were sharper than his social skills. "It's how I'm sure that's where I parked the car. I drove down a lane that was pretty muddy with that stuff last week, and it got plastered all over the undercarriage. It's been flaking off bit by bit."

"No way to identify the perp based on leftover mud then," Slade said with a playful tsk of his tongue. "Too bad. That would have made a good story."

"It could tell us where else the car's been once we start following the trail," Logan said, and rubbed his hands together. "Every clue matters."

Dexter was snapping more pictures, even though I wasn't sure how much he'd be able to make out in the increasingly dim light when he checked them later.

"I'd recognize the mud if I saw it again," I told him. "No pictures necessary."

He glanced back without actually meeting my eyes. "I like to keep a visual record. That way there's never any doubt. Memory is unreliable."

I guessed that was a fair point.

Slade tapped his lips. "We could still try to jog some memories. Find out who came through the lot last night and whether they noticed any suspicious characters."

"If anyone saw anything concerning, we'd already know about it," Logan said.

I raised an eyebrow at him. "How? Since when does the entire student body report to you?"

He shrugged. "We have our ways." He motioned to

the other guys, and Dexter straightened up, apparently done with his visual record-taking.

I was starting to get a sense of the dynamic between this group that called themselves "the Vigil": Logan taking the lead and making major judgment calls, Slade suggesting more out-of-the-box possibilities and stopping the tone from getting too dour, Dexter keeping track of the details.

They actually did feel like a cohesive unit, each bringing their own strengths, working together in well-practiced harmony. I might have enjoyed being a part of it if it hadn't been for my stepbrother's continued jerkishness.

Which Logan decided to demonstrate yet again just as that thought passed through my mind.

"If you had a nicer car, I'd say we start with resale sites and see if anyone's offering it, but your junker isn't going to fetch a high enough price to make it worthwhile for a thief to try to put it on the market like that."

"It's not a junker," I replied automatically. I'd bought it on my own dime when I'd started my first year of college so I could get to and from campus easily while I was still living at home, and I hadn't had enough money for anything fancy. It worked, and it got decent mileage. That was all that mattered.

How would Logan even know what type of car I drove? He'd already been long gone without a backward glance when I'd gotten it.

Logan snorted. "It is by car-buyer standards. How

much do you really think a 2006 Malibu is going to fetch? How much did *you* pay for it?" Before I could do more than sputter in response, he barreled onward, not waiting for an answer. "Whoever stole it would be best off selling it for parts. It's safer, and they'd get the most money that way."

Slade clapped his hands together. "Off to the chop shop, then! Darrel's our best bet." A hint of cinnamon wafted on his breath from the candy he was still rolling around his mouth.

"The chop shop?" I asked.

Logan looked at me like he'd forgotten I was here in the thirty seconds I'd stayed quiet. Like he wished I'd continued to stay quiet. But Slade gave me a wide smile.

"Chop shops are places that deal in stolen car parts behind a legit front," he said. "We know a guy who handles that kind of business out of his scrap yard."

I blinked at him. "You know a guy who's a criminal, and you just let him keep at it?"

Slade waved off my remark. "One of the first things you learn about solving crimes is that you need contacts. He isn't a bad guy. *He* doesn't steal anything. Every now and then he passes on a tip about other stuff that's going on around town, so we let him stick to his business as long as he isn't getting his nose too dirty."

"Right," Logan said brusquely, as if he resented that Slade had bothered to explain. "The scrap yard's open pretty late. We should head over there right now and get started tracking this thing down."

My spirits started to rise. At this point, there was no

way I was making it to the lecture I'd wanted to attend, but maybe I'd have my car back as soon as tonight. "Great. How are we getting there?"

Logan folded his arms over his broad chest. "There is no 'we,' not that includes you, anyway. You're not coming."

I scowled at him. "Why not? It's my car."

"Madelyn, we have a job to do, and it's better if we handle it alone, since we're the ones who actually know what we're doing. You can call an Uber to go for your trip to the mall or the hair salon or whatever you were planning on doing tonight."

Anger seared through me. Sure, I went to the mall and got my hair cut on occasion like most people did, but he made it sound like those were the only things I could have needed to do. Like I was a frivolous girl with nothing in her head but appearances.

What the hell was wrong with him? Even if he'd ghosted me for two years, he'd known me a heck of a lot better than that before. Why did he have to be such a gigantic asshole?

"For your information," I said tartly, "I was *planning* on driving to an in-depth talk in medical research developments, but it's too late for me to get there on time now. Which is too bad, because maybe I'd have learned something that'd help me figure out what *your* current damage is."

Logan's face twitched and hardened, and Dexter stood there awkwardly between him and me, looking at the cars rather than us.

Slade simply guffawed. "A brainiac. I like it." He gave my shoulder a playful knuckling and then swatted Logan. "Stop heckling the girl, man. She's clearly got her priorities straight."

I couldn't totally tell if it was a compliment or a backhanded insult.

"We need to get going before Darrel leaves the yard for the day," Dexter reminded his friends, looking down at the time on his phone.

Logan's jaw stayed clenched, and I set my hands on my hips. All kinds of other cutting remarks bubbled up in my chest, but I managed to hold them back by sheer force of will. *I need his help. I need his help.* I repeated the phrase like a mantra, hoping he wouldn't push me even farther. I wasn't sure I could stay even partly civil after much more dickishness.

"Dex is right," he said, drawing his already substantial frame even taller to glower down at me. "We have to get going. Just the three of us. Darrel knows us. He'd clam up around you anyway."

That didn't mean I couldn't ride with them so I could hear the outcome right away, but I guessed it was possible this chop-shop guy would notice me even then. I restrained a sigh and forced myself to nod.

I didn't want to ruin their chances of getting the answers I wanted. And the answers about the car *were* the most important ones, as much as I was dying to pummel Logan for an explanation of his behavior.

"Fine," I bit out. "But let me know what you find out as soon as you've talked to him." Dexter had exchanged phone numbers with me in a seemingly automatic gesture before we'd even come out here, which I guessed was standard procedure for them.

"Will do," Slade said with a jaunty salute.

The three guys strode off without a backward glance, leaving me alone in the parking lot, feeling totally useless.

CHAPTER
FIVE

Dexter

Normally I'd have welcomed a trip to the scrap yard. Darrel often had useful information to pass on that I could fit into my broader understanding of the criminal activities in this city. But Logan's silent brooding in the driver's seat left me with an unnerving sense of uncertainty.

I didn't understand his reaction to Madelyn at all. We'd all been surprised to see her, I was sure, and given the circumstances, it'd thrown us off balance. But Logan had seemed outright hostile. I had no idea where that animosity had come from.

It was true that he'd barely talked about her in a personal way in the past few years, but he'd always seemed fond of her back when they had socialized more. I'd never heard him say anything *negative* about her that would explain him treating her like an annoyance.

I didn't know much about her in general, of course —really only what Logan had said here and there in the early years of our friendship and observing her occasionally in the halls when we were in high school. So maybe there were factors I wasn't aware of. I hadn't found her annoying, though. She'd shown real determination, and she hadn't acted offended by my quirks the way people sometimes did.

I'd have thought Logan would have appreciated those qualities too. Definitely the determination part, anyway.

But the tension remained in my friend's shoulders through the entire drive. He drummed his fingers on the steering wheel and let out a huff of breath.

I bit back the urge to ask him what was going on. From past experience, I knew that asking a direct question about a subject that clearly discomforted him wouldn't get me a straight answer. Better to just watch and glean what I could as the situation played out.

There were other things I could ask that weren't likely to get his hackles up. I frowned as I thought over everything Madelyn had told us. "Do we think that the trinket box in Madelyn's car—the one that was her father's—was significant to the theft? Was it the real objective?"

Next to Logan, Slade stretched out his legs and cocked his head as he considered his answer. "From the way she described it, it didn't sound like anything all that exciting."

"I was thinking the same thing."

Slade flashed his typical grin at me. "Then I must be right."

Logan cleared his throat. "It's impossible to know how significant or not it is until we've seen the investigation through to the end. It's important to her, anyway. It was meaningful to him. Maybe it mattered to someone else too."

"Stranger things have happened," Slade said breezily, but he shot a sideways glance at Logan. It occurred to me that he'd noticed the other guy's tension too—and was doing his best to diffuse it. Slade was much better at that sort of thing than I was. "There *has* been a pattern of car thefts on campus, though. It's not like this was out of the blue."

"No," I said in exaggerated deadpan, "I believe they were red, black, silver, and now green."

Slade snorted, and even Logan cracked a bit of a smile. Humor might not be my specialty, but I'd learned that playing up my tendency to take things too literally could often get a laugh. Out of my friends, at least, since they caught the joke rather than thinking I was just confused.

"That's a good point, though," I went on, more seriously. "When we know there are already car thieves operating at the university, it's most likely to be just a random coincidence that they happened to target Madelyn's vehicle this time. Maybe they were hanging around in a good position to clone the fob at the worst possible moment for her."

"It's about time we took those pricks to task

anyway," Logan said. "Four cars in two months—that's a lot, and right under our noses in our main domain. We've got to shut the assholes down before people start to think the place is easy pickings under our watch."

"You've got to give Madelyn that much credit—she knew who to turn to." Slade shook his head. "Those other idiots taking the case to the city police, who of course just shot them back to useless Camp-Po. Their cars were probably long gone before anyone even really looked around for them. Man, I'd have given my other leg to have the chance to retrieve that red Mustang the one guy lost and take it for a little spin…"

Logan glanced at him, raising his eyebrows. "We wouldn't have been taking any stolen cars for a joyride."

"Don't tell me you wouldn't have wanted to. We both know that's utter bullshit." Slade cackled. "But I'd have been good and waited until the owner told us we could have a little fun, out of his utter gratitude. Wouldn't have been a bad thing to have a guy who can afford a Mustang owing us a favor either."

"Or whose family can afford a Mustang, at least," I said automatically.

"Yeah, yeah. Same difference."

"Well, we've already established he was an idiot," Logan said, but his voice sounded lighter now. "Favors are great, but rich idiots aren't. Anyway, we'll shut the thieves down and send them packing, and no one else will lose their precious vehicles or whatever they've stashed in them."

He spoke with a confidence I knew was justified.

Ever since we'd set up shop as the Vigil once we'd arrived at the university, where we were far enough away from our families that we weren't worried about how they'd react to our unusual "hobby" like we'd been in high school, we'd handled dozens of cases. We'd pretty much always figured out the source of the problem and dealt with it.

I wasn't totally sure why the other guys were so committed to our extracurricular activities, but for me piecing together those puzzles was absolutely exhilarating. It was a hell of a lot more enthralling than working through my Chemistry and Forensic Science coursework.

That involved puzzles too, but also a lot of busy-work, and most of it theoretical. Even the actual crimes we studied were ones already solved, just for practice. It was all leading to actual practice, of course, but with the Vigil, I didn't have to wait. I got to dig my hands right in and untangle the mysteries before anyone else had.

Still, as Logan pulled into the scrap yard's parking lot, a familiar knot formed in my stomach. I'd never meant for our quest for justice to become quite as intense as it had… but it was mostly my fault that we'd tumbled this far down the rabbit hole. Even if my friends never blamed me, I wasn't going to forget that fact.

"Darrel's still in," Logan said, tipping his head toward the small building just beyond the chain-link gate. Dusk was creeping over the yard, and light was glowing through the office window. "If these jerks are trying to get a major car theft ring going, they'd need to set up a connection with someone who can disassemble and move the parts quickly. Four cars just on campus— who knows how many they've grabbed around the city and other places nearby. There's a good chance he'll know what's up."

"If he wants to tell us," Slade said as we got out. "If they're paying *him*, he might not be so eager to pass on the information."

I glanced at the barbed-wire-topped fence, making out the vague shapes of ruined cars and other metal paraphernalia through the green mesh that stopped outsiders from scanning for details. "We'll be looking for clues at the same time. The other victims might not have come to us, but I know the makes and models of all four cars."

Slade reached out his hand as if to knuckle my shoulder but stopped just shy of touching me. If it'd been anyone other than him or Logan, I'd have flinched in anticipation of the contact, but my friends knew how to adapt their friendly gestures to my comfort levels.

"Of course you do," he said with amusement. "Let's go hunting."

We found the gate unlocked, like it usually was during business hours unless Darrel had some kind of private deal going on. As we eased inside, the unpleasant smell of heated metal and grease hit me. I wrinkled my nose.

The office door opened before we'd quite reached it, and Darrel's short, sinewy frame appeared in the doorway. He smiled broadly at us, showing off his one gold tooth amid the lightly yellowed natural ones. "Boys," he said in his boisterous voice that always struck me as a little too big for his body. "I was about to lock up, but I can make a little time for you. What've you come around to talk to me about today?"

He waved us into the office. We tramped inside, my skin prickling as the door thumped shut in our wake. I never totally liked being in an enclosed space with a known criminal, even one who'd proven as friendly as Darrel. You just couldn't be sure whether you'd stay on their good side.

Darrel gave Logan's arm a firm swat and leaned against his desk, still smiling. "Well, what's on your minds?"

The office was impressively neat, really, considering the chaotic heaps of parts that filled the rest of the scrap yard. Darrel himself kept his presentation orderly as well, wearing button-ups and slacks without a hint of a wrinkle, though I knew he swapped those out for tees and jeans when he was working the machines.

I wasn't totally sure what he made of our interest in tackling the criminals who ended up on our radar. We'd ended up on *his* radar last year after he'd inadvertently pissed off a fledgling gang who'd started harassing his customers in retaliation. We'd already been investigating the small group of amateur gangsters for other reasons, and after we'd confiscated some money to cover his lost business when we sent them packing, Darrel must have realized that the quest for justice could work in his favor as well as against it.

He had a sharp mind behind his warm demeanor, and I respected that. As long as he didn't outright hurt anyone to our knowledge, keeping a mutually beneficial alliance with him served our interests much better than trying to take him down for his own crimes.

Logan smiled back, smoothly but carefully. He knew as well as I did that associating with any kind of criminal was a dangerous balance. "We're actually wondering if business has been particularly good for you in the past couple of months. Gotten any exciting new clients?"

Darrel arched an eyebrow. He wasn't just going to blurt out his latest underworld associations. "What kind of exciting?"

"There's been a rash of car thefts on the university campus. The latest belonged to a friend of ours, and we're guessing the thieves would have been looking to sell it for parts. You're obviously the guy to go to for that kind of job. Naturally we wouldn't blame you for not realizing any particular vehicle had been stolen."

Despite the assurance, I noted the slight tightening of Darrel's posture. He knew that this case was taking us onto shaky ground, since he'd be a direct participant in the crimes we were looking into.

He didn't betray any other discomfort. "What's the make and model?" he asked. "I can tell you if anyone's tried to hawk it here or if I've heard talk around town."

And maybe he'd be telling the truth, or maybe he wouldn't.

"2006 Chevy Malibu," I said automatically. I'd filed away the details the moment Logan had said them and Madelyn hadn't disputed them.

It wasn't an outright piece of junk, but Logan's assessment of the car being close to worthless was confirmed by Darrel's snort. "Not exactly a luxury vehicle, then," he said. "I'm sorry, I haven't had any Chevys at all come through here recently."

I'd been worried that he might lie to us, but I found I had no doubt that his answer was genuine now that he'd given it. He'd obviously been amused at hearing the details, and the stiffness in his stance had relaxed as he'd answered. He was relieved that he didn't have anything to do with the crime. Possibly he honestly preferred not to lie to us now that we had a decent working relationship.

"These pricks obviously didn't know what they were doing then," Slade said with a chuckle.

Darrel echoed his laugh. "Maybe not. But I'm not the only option in this area—I may be the biggest provider of that particular service, but there are plenty of smaller chop shop operations in and around the city."

"I guess we'll have to start hitting up the other ones," Logan said. "I don't suppose there are any you figure are a particularly likely bet?"

Darrel made a face. "I don't really keep track of them—they're coming and going so often. If I do hear anything about a Malibu, I'll give you a call right away. Otherwise, I can't really help."

That time he wasn't being totally truthful. He was really saying that he *wouldn't* help us more than that. No doubt he knew of at least a couple of other active chop shops nearby, but it made sense that he wouldn't want to create bad blood for his business by pointing the finger if he really had no idea who might have handled this particular car.

"Well, thank you for your time," Logan said. "We always appreciate you lending your experience to our work."

As we headed back to the car, I surreptitiously snapped a few photos of the scrap yard with my phone. I'd gotten very good at taking pictures without looking like I was taking them in the years since we'd started our lives on this course, because having a concrete visual record was so valuable. Even in the thickening dark, the yard's security lights would show enough that it was worth documenting this visit.

We slid into the car in the same seats as before. I pretty much always ceded the front seat to Slade in consideration of his prosthetic, even though he insisted he didn't need special accommodations. Extra leg room couldn't *hurt*, and I didn't suffer without it. He was taller than me anyway.

Slade sighed and leaned his head back. "Now we need a new lead."

"We go to the smaller chop shops," Logan said. "One by one."

"Yeah, but that's going to take a lot more effort. They're not going to fill us in like Darrel did. It could take ages."

"It's strange that they aren't being brought here, isn't it?" I said slowly. "It seems like an ongoing operation with cars getting stolen regularly—wouldn't it make the most sense for them to set up an arrangement with the biggest chop shop in the area? Most of the smaller places wouldn't be able to hold many vehicles or parts at a time."

Slade popped one of the cinnamon candies he was hooked on into his mouth and clicked it against his teeth. "Maybe they aren't stealing anything except those cars on campus. A small chop shop could handle two a month. Or maybe they aren't all connected after all. Madelyn's could have been separate. We didn't ask him about the other three from before."

That was true. I'd automatically assumed that if Darrel hadn't handled Madelyn's car, he hadn't gotten any of them, but I shouldn't have.

If her Malibu had been specially targeted for reasons that had nothing to do with a general thieving operation, then this could be far bigger than just a stolen car. A quiver of anticipation rippled through the air between us.

"This is all just speculation," Logan said in his laying-down-the-law tone, starting the engine. "We follow the trail and see where it leads us. The one good thing about the smaller businesses is that they'd probably need longer to get around to breaking down a car. That gives us more time to find it before it's in pieces. First thing tomorrow, we'll start working through the suspects."

I rubbed my hands together, unable to ignore a deeper thrill that shot through me, both uneasy and eager.

Most of our jobs were minor puzzles, fairly easy to connect the dots. This was shaping up to be a real challenge. I couldn't wait to dive in… but I also had no idea what dark paths the case might lead us down.

CHAPTER
SIX

Madelyn

'd thought if I showed up at the law library first thing on Saturday morning, I might have a chance to poke around in the Vigil's office before any of the guys showed up—if they showed up at all. I knew from things Holand had said that Logan had an off-campus apartment he shared with his friends, and surely they had better things to do than hang out around school on the weekend.

As I tried the office door, grimacing to find it locked, my phone pinged with a text alert from my best friend and frequent co-conspirator Summer. I'd filled her in on my missing car and my interaction with the Vigil last night.

Normally, Summer would have been all for a little reconnaissance, only annoyed that she couldn't join in, since she'd ended up heading to Emerson College for its journalism program and was currently half a day's drive from me. But as soon as she'd found out Logan was involved, her tone had turned a lot more critical.

Tell me they found your car already so you can dump that jerk harder than he ditched you?

Summer had always had a strong sense of social justice, which was partly why we were such good friends. She'd been so pissed off when she'd found out how Logan had ghosted me after our hook-up that there'd been a solid three months where she never uttered his name, only referred to him as "the prick" or "the asshole" if he came up in conversation. Even these days, she mostly relied on insults.

Unfortunately, no, I wrote back. *They're still working on it.*

Well, let them do their thing and stay clear of him. I know you're curious, but he's not good for you.

I'm not going to do anything WITH him. I just want to know what's going on with him and this whole private investigator thing he's suddenly gotten into.

Unfortunately, Summer was very good at picking up on the things I wasn't saying. She sent a side-eyeing emoji with the question, *What are you doing, Maddie?*

Just trying to get into their office, I admitted. *Obviously none of them are going to tell me what all they've been doing, considering Logan hardly wanted to loop me in on the crime that affected me directly. It's totally justified snooping.*

I could almost hear her resigned sigh. *Well, I know nothing's going to get in your way once you're committed to a mission, girl. Just don't get too invested, all right? Or I'll be obligated to race on over there and rearrange his face when he hurts you again.*

I promise, I'm not giving him a chance. I learned my lesson.

Tucking my phone back into my pocket, I eyed the door. It wasn't as if I could pick the lock. How could I get my hands on a key?

It always irked me a little to play the desperate girl, but sadly being female and upset opened doors—sometimes literally—when nothing else would. I hurried over to the reception desk as if I were a little frantic and came to a stop in front of the librarian on duty, pressing my hands against the check-out counter. "I'm so sorry, but I could really use some help."

The librarian peered at me through her round glasses and offered a sympathetic smile. "I'm here to assist however I can. Is there a particular book you're looking for?"

"No," I said with an awkward wave toward the back of the room. "I just—I came to see the Vigil the other night, and I realized afterward that I left a binder in their office. I need the notes in it to study for a test on Monday, and I don't know if they're going to be back all weekend. Could you possibly let me in for just a minute so I can find it?"

It might not buy me *much* time, but at least I could take a closer look around while I pretended to search for my supposed binder.

The librarian's smile faded. "I'm sorry. I have an

agreement with the boys that they have sole use of that space, and I know there are a lot of private matters that they handle for other students. I have their numbers if you need to give them a call and see if they'd let you in?"

Crap. Now I had to go along with her offer, or it'd be obvious I'd been lying. "Sure. Thank you so much."

I jotted down the numbers she gave me and walked away as if to place my call in private. Over at the back of the library where the Vigil room was, she couldn't see me anyway. I studied the solid wood door again, wondering if there was any chance I could just jiggle the lock open—ha ha ha. Maybe in my dreams.

I grasped the knob again just in case it'd only been stuck before rather than being actually locked, and just my luck, a low, teasing voice carried to my ears at the same moment.

"We tend to use the key to make it a little easier to get inside."

I whipped toward the male voice that'd come from behind me, and there, standing just a few feet away, was Slade, dangling a key from one hand while he grinned at me.

"I—" How would I explain this to him? The last thing I needed was for both Logan and Slade to believe I was a creepy stalker lady. I settled for avoiding the subject completely. "I imagine that *would* make it easier. Thank you."

Slade stepped past me to insert the key into the lock. He glanced over his shoulder at me. "I thought

Dexter passed on a message to you last night that we haven't located your car yet."

"Oh, well, yeah, but he didn't say much." That was my perfect excuse right there. "I was hoping to find out more, or that you might have made some more progress since then." I splayed my hands in what I hoped looked like a cluelessly innocent gesture, although I hated playing clueless even more than I hated doing the desperate female act.

"I'm sorry, but we haven't really had time." Slade pushed open the door and stepped inside. He paused for a second before grinning at me and beckoning me to follow. "I know Logan gave you kind of a hard time. Don't take it personally. He's got a lot on his mind. If you have more questions about how we'll handle the investigation, ask away."

I hadn't wanted to get into the office while one of the Vigil members was present, but if it was going to be anyone, I guessed Slade was the one least likely to give me a hard time. Maybe I could still find something out. And I could poke around a bit without looking suspicious, just curious.

He stood to the side of the door, popping one of those candies he seemed very fond of into his mouth. As I walked in, I caught a whiff of cinnamon and the click of it against his teeth.

"What exactly happened yesterday?" I asked. "You went to that chop shop place, right?"

"Of course." Slade dropped into one of the scattered chairs and leaned back, propping his feet on the edge of the table in a way that made the leg of his khakis slide up to reveal the metal rod of his prosthetic. Just like I remembered from high school, he showed no sign of self-consciousness. He might even have been showing it off purposefully to see if I'd react to it.

"Turns out your thief wasn't a customer of that particular shop," he went on in a casual tone. "He must have taken it someplace else. Or he knew someone with a special hankering for an old Malibu. We'll figure out which. It'll just take a little time to get through all the possibilities."

"That makes sense." I'd meant to start my perusal of the office, but Slade chose that moment to tuck his hands behind his head, making the muscles in his arms and shoulders flex to impressive effect. For a second, I found it hard to drag my gaze away from his dark, twinkling eyes and well-built body.

Slade wasn't as brawny as Logan, but he had an impressive physique in his own right. And those sly eyes combined with his bright grin and his carefree personality had drawn girls to him like bees to nectar back in high school. I recalled Summer catcalling him in the halls once when he'd been showing off his nimbleness on that manufactured leg, back when we'd been measly sophomores to his superior junior status.

I wasn't here to pursue a hookup, let alone anything more than that. I didn't want to feel the twang of desire that shot through me before I finally yanked my eyes away—but I'd be lying if I said it hadn't happened.

I had more important things to focus on right now.

And the last thing I needed was to get a crush on Logan's best friend.

Wandering around the table, I let my fingers trail over the surface, shifting a few of the papers lying there to an angle that made them easier for me to read. A quick glance showed nothing all that exciting: a class schedule for a student whose name I didn't recognize, a sketch that didn't look like much more than a few overlapping rectangles to me, a recent receipt for a video game. I wasn't sure whether the last was evidence or just one of the Vigil guys' personal purchases.

"Are you sure that you *will* be able to track down my car now that you're on the case?" I asked.

Slade tsked his tongue. "Don't be doubting us already. We've got a reputation to maintain here—we'll get it done."

I couldn't help raising my eyebrows at him. "You're awfully confident. How long have you guys been at this whole Vigil thing anyway?"

He shrugged. "Since pretty soon after we started classes here, so about two and a half years now."

Honest curiosity itched at me. "How did you even get started doing something like this? Most people don't suddenly decide, 'Hey, I'm going to become a crusader tackling all the crimes on campus.'"

Slade's grin stretched wider. "You should know something about being a crusader, shouldn't you, Madelyn?"

The lilt with which he said my name sounded almost flirty—enough to make me blush. Or maybe that was just residual embarrassment being reminded of my many crusades in high school.

Not that I was ashamed of the stands I'd taken… but I could definitely have tackled certain conflicts with a more polished approach.

"I asked you the question first," I retorted.

Slade laughed. "Fair. It's not that thrilling a story, as much as I'd like to wow you with grand tales of derring-do. We actually picked up a few sort-of cases back in high school. Opportunities landed in our lap, and we found that we were good at putting pieces together and figuring out the solutions to these kinds of problems. We did little investigations like the kids we were, and when we came here, we decided to make more of a commitment to getting shit done."

I blinked at him, momentarily forgetting my quest to unravel what they were up to now in my surprise about the past. "You were solving crimes back in high school?"

"Sure. We just kept it more on the down-low then. Lots of other things keeping us occupied. Remember the English teacher Miss Otterbine?"

At my nod, he continued. "Well, someone stole the mini-refrigerator she kept in her room, and she couldn't go to the school about it because technically the appliance wasn't allowed outside of the teachers' lounge. She only had it in there to keep backup lunches for students who couldn't afford them. So we decided to find out who'd taken off with it, and we did. She got her fridge back, and the culprit got a very stern talking-to." He winked at me.

I opened my mouth to ask for more details about their high-school exploits, which had gone on right under my nose, but Slade whipped his feet off the table and straightened up, fixing me with an intent look. "So, Maddie—do you mind if I call you Maddie?"

I got a weird twinge thinking of how natural it sounded from his mouth—and how natural it'd used to sound from Logan's. "Go for it," I said.

"What are *you* occupying yourself with these days? You said you were going to some medical research lecture—am I right in thinking you're pre-med?"

I was a little surprised that he'd remembered that brief part of our conversation last night—but then, he had come to my defense when Logan had been hassling me about my plans.

"You've got it," I said. "I'm majoring in biology." I paused. I knew Logan had gone into something to do with computers—his dad talked about it now and then with a note of pride, since he had enough trouble wrangling anything outside of his accounting software— but I had no idea about his friends. "What about you?"

"World languages with a specialty in linguistics."

My eyebrows rose. "World languages as in plural? Don't people usually pick just one?"

His chuckle resonated through the room. "I might look like a jock, but I *do* know languages. I got English and Spanish from home, and I taught myself a fair amount of Italian and French all on my own, enough to be fluent now."

I gaped. "You know *four* languages?"

"Don't sound so surprised, Piccolina," he said. "After you know two or three, the rest get easier. Mandarin and Russian were a more difficult challenge, since they're not under the Romance umbrella—that means based on Latin, not swoony romance, although I excel in the latter too." He shot me a smile that made me absolutely certain he was flirting with me. "Hĕn gāoxìng jiàn dào nǐ? Vasha siyayushchaya ulibka voshishchayetsya dazhe nebom!"

He switched between the two languages without missing a beat, sounding totally comfortable with both. "Six languages," I muttered, hardly able to believe my ears.

"Eight if you count Tagalog and Arabic, but I'm not proficient in those yet. Those are my current projects."

Okay, clearly there was a lot going on behind that handsome face that I hadn't realized. I only knew *one* language, unless you counted the wide assortment of scientific terms I'd had to add to my vocabulary, which thankfully didn't require their own grammatical rules or anything like that.

The thought of how much I hadn't known about Slade brought my mind back to the mysteries surrounding Logan—and my main reason for being here. I pulled myself away from the table and meandered farther into the office as if aimlessly checking the place out. "And Logan's doing computer science and engineering, right?"

"You should know."

Should I? I kept my voice as even as I could manage. "A double major like that has got to be intense. Is that what's got him on edge?"

"Ah, he's a natural at that stuff, so I doubt he has any more trouble with it than you do with your biology work."

That wasn't much of a question, but there was a firmness to the words that hadn't been there before. I could tell if I tried to push further, Slade would only deflect me. His loyalty was to Logan, not me, of course. I could hardly expect him to spill his best friend's secrets.

I forced a laugh, letting my gaze skim over the computer desk. They hadn't left anything out around the computer other than a takeout menu that I suspected was for their own benefit, not an investigation. "It's been a bit of a challenge adjusting to the slightly different curriculum here, transferring in the middle of the year, but I'm getting back into the groove."

Slade cocked his head. "That's right—this is the first semester I've seen you around campus. You finally followed us here, huh? Missed being in the presence of the great Slade Galvezo that much?"

My next laugh came out more genuine. "I always wanted to come here—well, since I first started thinking about college, before any of you got accepted anywhere.

But I didn't get in at first—I had to start at the community college back home."

It was Slade's turn to arch his eyebrows in shock. "You weren't accepted? A smarty-pants like you?"

I wrinkled my nose at him. "I might have been smart in certain ways, but I didn't handle school politics all that brilliantly. There was this one teacher— American History—he was always playing favorites: offering bonus assignments only to the students who'd joined the comics club he ran, giving them extra time on tests, that kind of thing. It drove me crazy. So I stood up to him, started calling him out loudly in class, and he hated me after that. Suddenly all my essays were getting Ds. I nearly failed the class, and it tanked the GPA I needed."

Slade let out a low whistle. "I do seem to remember you being a bit of a hardass back in high school. Not that there's anything wrong with that. Sometimes jerks like that need to be put in their place."

"Yeah, well, it lost me three semesters here for my trouble. I'm not saying he didn't deserve it, but I'd have gone about it a little differently if I'd thought things through more ahead of time."

"It's too bad we weren't still around to get on his case and prove he was screwing you over." Slade shook his head and tapped his prosthetic foot against the floor with an emphatic *thunk*.

The artificial limb drew my attention again. I paused, a sudden memory tickling up through my mind —but should I say anything?

Well, Slade seemed like the type to tell me off without batting an eye if I deserved it. "Would it be horribly rude if I say something about your leg?" I asked, lifting my chin toward him.

Slade waved off any concerns I'd had. "I'm curious to hear your thoughts, Dr. Maddie. Should I tell you about the awful shark attack and how I harpooned the beast that chomped it off?"

I gave him a baleful look at the obvious joke. "I was just thinking—I follow a lot of different areas of medical research, just to stay on top of new developments. There are some teams that've been making a lot of progress with new types of prosthetics with robotic elements and things like that."

"Becoming part robot? Sounds interesting."

I couldn't tell if he was making fun of the idea or honestly intrigued, but I barreled onward. "Some of the companies are looking for volunteer amputees to beta test the parts. I'm not sure if it's something that would interest you since you're so good with the prosthetic you already have. It's not like you need the help of fancy gadgets. But if you thought it'd be worth giving a shot, I can always point you in the right direction."

Slade stared at me for a long moment, his expression suddenly impossible to read. I hoped I hadn't pissed him off with the suggestion despite his reassurances, especially when my intention had been the exact opposite.

Then his lips curved with a warm smile that met his eyes. The teasing note dropped from his voice for just a moment. "That's a pretty fantastic offer. I'd be happy to become an even more spectacular cyborg. Thank you, Piccolina."

I crossed my arms over my chest. "What does that mean?"

"It means that I appreciate the gesture." He motioned me back toward him. "I'd be happy to look into it. I'll give you my number, and you can text me the deets—or, y'know, if you're ever in the mood for a booty call…"

He smirked so widely with that last remark that I couldn't help laughing. "I'm not really the booty-call type, but I'm very flattered. I can send you the info, for sure."

I passed him the phone and gave the room another scan while he fiddled with it. My gaze latched on to the filing cabinet I hadn't checked yet. I sauntered over and gave the top drawer a little tug.

It jarred without opening—locked, presumably. I tried the second drawer down with the same result. Before I could reach for the third, Slade's voice, calm but suddenly much more serious, carried across the room.

"That's where we keep case files. Gotta make sure no one else gets in there, or it'd violate our clients' confidentiality. Don't worry, we're just as careful with your info too."

Guilt heated my cheeks. "I'm sorry. I didn't realize —I wasn't really thinking."

That last part was a lie, but I didn't want him to

think of me as a snoop. Somehow that seemed even more important than before I'd ended up chatting with him. I'd kind of liked our rambling conversation, I realized. I hadn't felt that relaxed simply shooting the breeze with a guy in… ages. Maybe forever. Even when Logan and I had been friendly, there'd always been my crush in the back of my mind, making me nervous. Slade had a way of putting people at ease.

Like now. His smile returned in the blink of an eye, so swiftly it was hard to believe he'd sounded so intense a moment ago.

He got up and handed my phone back to me. As I took it, he slipped his arm around me to touch the small of my back, nudging me toward the door. "It's no problem. You just never know what suspicious characters we'll need to protect our inside info from, especially when it comes to pretty girls who give away their numbers for potential booty calls."

I snorted and elbowed him playfully, but I let him usher me toward the door. It seemed like he'd decided I'd spent enough time in the Vigil's domain, and I had no excuses left to keep me there. I'd checked out everything I could with him watching over me anyway.

"Keep up those studies," he said as I stepped out into the library's main room. "We'll be in touch as soon as we find out anything about your car."

I nodded and only offered a small wave as he closed the door in my face, the lock clicking behind him. As I headed out of the building, my thoughts started to whirl in my head.

Slade had seemed perfectly content to chat casually with me until I'd touched that filing cabinet. Then suddenly he hadn't been able to get me out of the office fast enough, even if he'd still been flirting his ass off the whole time.

It wasn't as if I could have seen any of the confidential files while the drawers were locked anyway. Just what were the guys hiding in there that had prompted such a strong reaction?

CHAPTER
SEVEN

Logan

I spotted Dad's car in the parking lot as I pulled up to the diner, even though I'd arrived fifteen minutes early. How long had he been waiting inside for me already? Was he that intent on squeezing every possible second he could get out of our lunches together?

It sounded like something he would do. And I couldn't even blame him. It wasn't as if I gave him all that much of my time these days.

A pang of guilt ran through my chest, but I shook it off. The distance was necessary for his good as much as mine. Maybe even more his. If I hadn't thought it'd send him into a panic, I'd have forced myself to cut him off completely.

There was no reason that the darker side of my life should ever have to infect his.

My smartwatch vibrated on my wrist. Without even

looking at it, I reached into my glove compartment where I kept one of my various stashes of pills. It was better to have them on hand wherever I happened to be, since the timing was important.

I tossed back the single pill I was down to with a gulp of water, suppressing my irritation. It sucked being chained to this routine, knowing that my survival depended on following it. The doctors had said I might be able to wean off the immunosuppressants completely one day, that there were other liver transplant recipients who'd managed it without major issues, but so far they hadn't felt confident enough at my periodic check-ups to give me the go-ahead.

I might be willing to take a lot of risks, but messing around with the extension I'd already been lucky to get on my natural expiration date wasn't one of them.

Taking the pill only took a moment, and then I could pretend to forget that anything about me was remotely broken—at least physically—until the next time that alarm went off.

I gave myself another several seconds to gather the good spirits I'd need to show Dad to make sure he didn't have a panic attack even though he *was* seeing me, and then stepped out of the car. The greasy smell of the diner's decadent burgers wafted through the parking lot as I headed for the door.

It wasn't my favorite restaurant, but Dad loved it— and it was continuing a tradition we'd established a few years after my transplant when my health had settled into a sort of equilibrium. Once a month, Dad would take me out for a "cheat meal"—something fatty or greasy or sugary that the doctors wouldn't have approved of as a regular part of my diet. Just an occasional treat, a reminder that I didn't have to give those indulgences up completely.

I'd savored those moments as a kid. These days, it didn't matter as much to me, but it made Dad happy. So I went along with it. It was one little gift I could give him. I sure as hell owed him something.

Warmth washed over me on my way into the diner. It was a small space, room for maybe thirty people around eight tables at full capacity. Retro Coca-Cola signs and records hung on the walls. It was old-school in operation too—you had to go to the counter to order, and then the server would bring the meal to your table and take care of things from there. I paused just long enough to ask for my usual and point out where I'd be sitting.

Dad was seated at our usual table at the back near one of the windows, his hands cupped around a mug of steaming coffee. I strode over, pushing my mouth into a smile, forcing my mind to empty of all the things I couldn't tell him.

We'd have long conversations—we always did—but I wouldn't mention anything about the Vigil or my recent extracurriculars. My dad would know me as a hard-working engineering student and nothing more. I could tell him about my midterms, about hanging out with Slade and Dexter when we weren't getting into trouble, and about the overall campus life. That was it.

That was how it had to be.

Dad's head came up at my approach, and he beamed at me so brightly that a sharper pang reverberated through me. He loved me so goddamn much, but he had no idea who I even was these days.

He slid out of the booth and opened his arms to me, and I allowed him to wrap me in his embrace. I hugged him back, giving myself over to the show of affection just for a moment.

I owed him this too. And part of me welcomed the gesture even if it made me uncomfortable at the same time.

Every time we hugged, I felt as if his arms had shrunk and mine expanded. I was a little taller than him now and definitely bulkier from my regular workouts. Did he even notice, or did he still feel like he was hugging the little boy I used to be?

Did he believe that he knew the man he hugged? From where I stood, he didn't. He barely knew a thing about me anymore.

"Always good to see you, bud," he said as he released me, still smiling away. "I'm glad we can still make time for these get-togethers."

"Always," I assured him. I sat down across from him, focusing all my thoughts on the subjects it was safe to talk about. "How've you been? Is the merger still working out okay?" His accounting firm had recently absorbed another smaller company, and Dad had spent some time running around getting everyone settled into the new organizational structure. I didn't think it was really part of his job, but he was the kind of guy who couldn't help making sure everyone was at ease.

"Oh, everyone seems pretty comfortable now," Dad said, sounding pleased. "Those kinds of transitions are always tough at first, but we've brought on some really great talent. And we made it through the busiest part of tax season without anyone having a nervous breakdown, so that's always a win." He winked at me to show he was joking about the breakdown thing. "Did you wrap up that big engineering project?"

I nodded. "Turned in my papers last week. Haven't gotten them back yet, but I feel good about how it came together. I used a lot of the concepts the prof's been harping on, so he should be impressed anyway."

The truth was that I didn't care all that much about my studies other than how they could help advance my other activities, but keeping the authorities at school happy meant they didn't examine those other activities too closely.

Dad chuckled. "Always smart to play to the teacher's interests. Good for you." He paused, turning the mug in his hands. "I was just telling Lindsay about the sorts of things you've been working on, and I realized I couldn't explain most of the details. She's got more of a mind for the science and tech stuff than I do. Someday you'll have to fill her in properly."

It was a subtle hint that he'd like me to stop by the house—sooner rather than later—and reconnect with more of the family. As much as I could consider the stepmother I'd gotten at sixteen years old a family member, even if Madelyn's mom was the best thing that'd happened to my dad since Mom's death years before. But Dad knew better than to push too hard, and his hints were easy to ignore as if I hadn't caught his full meaning.

"The next time I see her, I'll give her the full scoop," I said noncommittally. The next time I saw her would quite possibly not be until next Christmas, but I didn't have to clarify that.

"She'll enjoy hearing about it." Dad tapped the top of the table. "I hope you've been making time for things other than work, though. You should have the full college experience, fit some fun into that busy schedule of yours."

Oh, I did… if you could consider chatting up criminals, interrupting gang operations, and investigating thefts "fun." Sometimes it kind of was.

"Don't worry, Dad," I said. "I'm doing a lot more than just studying."

"Don't get me wrong," he said. "I'm impressed that I raised such a smart one. Your mother would have been so proud of you too, you know."

I nodded, my throat tightening a little. Dad could talk about Mom without getting emotional these days, and generally I could too. But when I thought about the two of them…

After I'd gotten sick, even after the transplant that'd ultimately saved my life, things between them had seemed increasingly strained. I couldn't help thinking the stress of my treatments had fractured their marriage.

I couldn't say I was sure they'd have stayed together much longer if we hadn't lost Mom to that accident when I was ten.

"Anyway, my point is just that it's important to remember balance." Dad reached across the table to pat my arm. "You have your studies and your friends and your health and whatever you do to relax and enjoy yourself—and of course family."

He shot me one of those warm grins, and my returning smile got stiffer. That was another hint, one even easier to ignore but that jabbed me all the same.

"That's why I'm glad we have these lunches every month," I said in my best enthusiastic tone.

"Speaking of family..." Dad paused when the waitress came over with our orders: burgers and fries, mine with pickles and raw onions, Dad's slathered in cheese and mayo. My heart had started to sink at his words, and the interruption wasn't enough to get me out of the new turn in the conversation. Dad popped a fry into his mouth, gave a happy sigh, and fixed his attention on me again. "Have you seen Maddie around campus much since she transferred over?"

I shrugged and bit into my burger to buy myself some time while I rode out the surge of emotions that came up at the mention of the girl—no, the *woman* now—who'd been way too present in my mind for the past couple of days. The meaty juices mingled with the tang of the onion and pickles, but I couldn't take much enjoyment from the meal.

"You know, we're in pretty different fields," I said.

"It's a big campus. I'd never see Slade or Dexter there if I didn't arrange to meet up with them."

I knew as soon as the words came out of my mouth that I'd made a misstep. Dad waved a fry at me. "You should get in touch with her—text her or video chat or whatever you kids do instead of calling people like a normal human being these days—and offer to show her around. You've got to know the campus a lot better than she does."

I raised my eyebrows at him, pretending amusement. "Dad, she's been at the school for what? Three months? I think she's figured out her way around by now."

"Still, I'm sure it'd be nice for you two to reconnect. You were friendly back in school before Lindsay and I ever got together, weren't you? And you always got along well after too."

"Yeah," I said quietly. Until I'd had to retreat from every part of my old life that I didn't want to put under threat.

What would he say if he knew just how thoroughly we'd "reconnected." I was handling a fucking case for her. I'd seen more of her yesterday than I had in the entire three years since I'd moved out of her mom's house. Way too much for comfort...

And also nowhere near as much as a different part of myself wished it'd been. But that was the biggest problem right there.

I couldn't act on those urges. I'd already screwed things up enough once, getting caught up in the moment and then having to cut her out again cold turkey. I could only imagine how hurt and angry she'd been… I'd seen those emotions simmering behind her eyes every time she'd looked at me when we'd been talking about nothing but her stupid car.

The memory made me wince inwardly, a sharp ache lancing through my chest. I'd hurt her badly. After she'd patched me up, touched me so tenderly, opened herself up to me…

But she could get hurt so much worse if she got tangled up in the life I had now. We'd find her car, figure out if there was anything significant about the box, and then fade right back off her radar as if she and I had never spoken.

I wouldn't bring her anything but trouble if I stuck around, which she should have figured out in spades after our last collision.

"I did give her a few tips when she first arrived," I said, just to get Dad off the subject.

It was a bald lie, but he took it as the truth without hesitation. As easily as I'd told the lie in the first place.

It was awful, wasn't it, how easy and even automatic bullshitting the man who'd raised me had become? That I'd become the kind of guy who lied to his loving dad?

But that was the trade-off I'd taken. I'd gotten a lot more of a childhood than I'd been meant to after I got sick; I'd gotten to live, period. Now I was paying back the second chance I'd been granted thanks to someone else's death by helping people in ways even the cops couldn't.

I should be grateful for as much normalcy as I'd gotten before the path I'd started down had turned dangerous. Now all that mattered was protecting the people I cared about, and if that meant keeping them as far away from me as possible, so be it.

If only doing that had stayed simpler to accomplish when it came to Madelyn.

"I'm glad to hear it," Dad said. "That girl's got one of the biggest hearts out there." As if I didn't already know that. But thankfully, he shifted to a different topic. "Hey, are you still following the Red Sox these days? Quite the game on Saturday."

"Yeah," I said, though I'd only caught the highlights, and slid back into the meaningless chatter that couldn't hurt anyone or anything. Beneath my offhand remarks, a sense of resolve had solidified in my gut.

We needed to get that car theft solved *yesterday* so I could shove Madelyn as far away from me as I could—and make sure she stayed away this time.

CHAPTER
EIGHT

Madelyn

A knock jolted me out of the zone of concentration I'd gotten into as I typed out the finishing touches to my latest Genetics assignment at my desk. When I glanced toward the door, Keeley did too, popping out her earphones that'd been buzzing the voices of her favorite podcast while she paged through a textbook. I had no idea how she managed to focus with people yammering right in her ears, but she said it actually helped her.

Her desk was a little closer, and she was the one of us much more likely to be receiving visitors anyway. She jumped up and opened the door with a curious expression that told me she hadn't been expecting anyone.

To my surprise, I caught sight of a familiar face beyond her. Dexter Wright was standing awkwardly in the residence hallway, clutching the strap of a satchel that hung from his shoulder. He blinked at Keeley and then aimed his gaze at me for a second before it darted away from both of us in typical Dexter style.

Keeley tilted her head to the side, twisting one of her curls around a finger. "Hello, there. Can I help you?"

She'd taken on a playfully flirty tone that made me reevaluate the situation—and the guy beyond the door. Keeley obviously thought he was cute. I guessed he was, if I let myself think about it. His dark curls and pale skin made his large green eyes look even more vivid in contrast, and even though he was slim, you could tell he had some lean muscle on him.

The Vigil probably had girls falling over them all across campus. What a group.

Of course, Dexter wasn't so great with the smooth charm Slade had in abundance. He made a vague motion in my direction. "I'm here to talk to Madelyn," he said, firmly and evenly.

"Oh, are you?" Keeley cooed, and peeked over her shoulder to waggle her eyebrows at me. I barely restrained myself from rolling my eyes in return, since Dexter would see and might get the wrong idea. This wasn't some kind of hookup, but I didn't want him to think I was annoyed that he'd come by. Keeley just had an overactive imagination... and a theory that I really needed to get laid sometime before the end of the semester.

Keeley stepped aside to motion Dexter into the

small room and then scooted past him. "I'll leave you two alone," she informed us, flashing me another suggestive smile. "I can make myself scarce for a good long time. Total privacy. Have fun!"

Oh, God. My cheeks flared.

Dexter peered after my roommate's retreating back with a puzzled expression for the moment before the door thumped shut. Then he glanced around the room, his stance tensing as he took in the two somewhat rumpled beds that were the only furniture other than the desk I was already occupying and Keeley's.

"I'm sorry," I said, feeling as awkward as he looked. "She's very… exuberant. She's just trying to be a good friend. Is this about my car?"

Dexter nodded, catching my eyes for half a second before his gaze started traveling around the room again. "I had a few things to talk to you about, and this seemed like the most likely place to find you."

"You could have just texted me."

He shrugged. "I needed something you could only do in person. If you hadn't been here, then I would have texted."

I guess that made some sort of sense. When he glanced around again, adjusting his weight on his feet, I sprang out of my chair. Of course he'd feel weird sitting on my *bed*, for fuck's sake, especially after how Keeley had just been acting.

"Here," I said. "You can sit at my desk. What exactly did you need to go over? Have you made any progress?" It didn't seem probable that they'd accomplished much in the ten or so hours since I'd talked to Slade this morning.

I sat down on my bed, tucking my legs up so that Dexter could walk by easily. He seemed to relax a bit as he sank into my desk chair. He turned it toward me and pulled a thin pad of paper and a pencil out of his satchel. His gaze held mine again for only a second before it dropped to more like the vicinity of my mouth.

"We'd like you to draw the box that was in your car—so we'll be able to describe it accurately if we need to ask around about it."

Okay, that seemed reasonable enough. I accepted the pad and pencil and sketched out the rough rectangular shape. It wasn't a work of art, but then, I didn't think they expected it to be.

"So, I take it you haven't found the car yet," I said dryly.

Dexter didn't seem to pick up on the intended humor in my statement. "No, we haven't. But as I mentioned last night, we determined that it hasn't been taken to the largest chop shop in the area. And Logan confirmed this morning that it wasn't used in any crime that's been reported."

I blinked at him. "Used in a crime?" I repeated in confusion.

Dexter nodded, looking more at my shoulder now. "Stolen for a joyride and then abandoned, or reported as a getaway vehicle in a robbery, or anything like that."

"And how would he have confirmed that?"

Another brief moment of eye contact. "He hacked into the police department's database."

My pencil paused where I'd started to draw the Celtic knot on the top of the trinket box from memory. I gaped at Dexter. "He can do that?"

I'd known Logan was good with computers—obviously, since he was a computer science major—but I'd had no idea he'd delved into hacking. And hacking into a network I'd imagine had to be pretty secure, considering it was law enforcement. He had asked his dad for quite the elaborate computer set up back in high school, but I'd assumed he'd wanted the latest tech for gaming.

How much else had he been hiding from me and the rest of the family?

Dexter nodded as if it were no big deal. Maybe to him it wasn't. "Sure. That's one of the ways we follow the trails of clues."

Well, I guessed I had a better idea now of how the Vigil managed to solve crimes the cops couldn't. I was pretty sure the police didn't have any hackers on staff.

I directed my attention at the paper again, drawing the curves of the Celtic knot as well as I could remember them. Then I passed the sketch over to Dexter. "That's about what it looks like. Nothing too fancy, like I said."

Dexter examined the drawing and tucked it into his bag. "Thank you."

"Is that what you're going to do next?" I asked. "Start asking around?"

"With a little more direction than that," Dexter said. "We need to determine what smaller chop shops are currently active in the city, since they're hiding behind fronts, and check them all out."

"Will that take a lot of time?"

"It depends on luck, really, unfortunately. We're going to touch base with a contact or two tonight who might be able to point us in the right direction."

I immediately perked up. "I'll come along too, then. I know my car way better than any of you. I should hear what these contacts have to say."

Dexter tensed up all over again. His gaze slid to the floor, and his mouth opened and closed a few times before he seemed to find his words. "I don't think that's a good idea."

Guilt pinched my gut at how uncomfortable I'd made him, but I squared my shoulders. I'd promised myself I wouldn't back down. Logan had probably sent Dexter on this mission because he'd figured I'd be too much of a softie to put pressure on his shy friend. He wasn't putting me off that easily.

"I'm not asking," I said, standing up. "I'm insisting. You guys shut me out last night, but I want to be a part of the investigation. It's my property that got stolen, after all."

Dexter spread his hands awkwardly. "Madelyn… It's not that simple…"

"Sure it is. As long as you're not letting Logan boss you around, which I don't intend to do. You don't have to make the call. Bring me to the other guys wherever you're meeting up, and I'll make my case with them."

Dexter shook his head. "I'm not bringing you to the apartment. No one goes there except the three of us. That's the rule."

Not even casual hookups, which it'd sounded like Slade at least was keen on? Interesting. I folded my arms over my chest. "Fine. Then call them and tell them to come to campus, and I'll talk to them here."

Dexter hesitated, his posture painfully rigid. I swallowed hard, knowing he was straining his mind for a way to get out of this—a way to convince me to back off. He needed to understand that wasn't an option.

Did he have a specific problem with me, or was it just because of Logan's objections? Well, it didn't matter either way.

"Look," I said quietly, "I know there was some drama around taking my case. I realize Logan's been a jerk about it. But this is my car, my memento of my dad. It's my *life*. I won't get in anyone's way or screw things up, but I want to be as much a part of the investigation as I can be. Isn't that a reasonable request?"

Dexter's mouth twisted, and then he let out a brisk exhalation. "I'll text them. But I don't think Logan will be happy."

A sly smile curved my lips. "You don't have to tell them I'll be there. Let me handle Logan."

Dexter looked skeptical, but he tapped out a message on his phone. A moment later, an answering ping carried through the room. He glanced at the screen and then shoved the phone back in his pocket. "They'll be in the parking lot outside the main library in ten minutes."

He got up, not looking at me but not objecting when I followed him. I kept a careful distance as we walked through the hall and down the stairs, not wanting to push into his personal space.

From the brief observations I'd made of Dexter back in high school, I knew he wasn't the touchy-feeling type. I'd seen him flinch from as simple a gesture as a guy giving him a friendly clap on the shoulder. He'd always stood a little farther back from any group he was part of than the others.

He'd done me a favor, and the least I could do was keep his comfort in mind in every way I could that didn't jeopardize my own goals.

As we stepped out of the residence building, a gust of cool spring air whacked me in the face. It'd been pretty warm by daylight, but any lingering heat had died with the setting sun. Dexter strode a little ahead of me on his long legs, and I hurried to keep up as we headed along the darkened concrete paths toward the larger of the campus libraries.

Just as we came around the looming brick building to where the parking lot lay, Logan's car, a black Subaru, cruised into the space, headlights streaking through the dusk. Logan parked near us, and I could already tell from his face through the windshield that he was pissed.

He and Slade both got out, Slade leaning against the

side of the car with an amused air and Logan marching a few steps toward us. "What's *she* doing here?"

"She wants to come with us," Dexter said before I needed to explain.

Logan snorted, and my hands clenched at my sides.

"I *am* coming with you," I clarified, ignoring Logan and walking over to his Subaru. "My case, my car. I'd like to see exactly what you're doing to find it."

Logan's eyes turned even icier than before. "You're going to get in our way and make a nuisance of yourself. Go back to your dorm." He motioned to Dexter as he turned back to the car. "Come on, let's get going before she wastes any more of our time."

That last comment stung. My jaw set, and without really thinking about what I was doing, I strode forward even faster. Before Logan had quite made it to the driver's side door, I'd reached the hood. Without missing a beat, I clambered right up onto it and plopped myself down in front of the windshield.

"What the hell are you doing?" Logan snapped.

I crossed my arms over my chest and glowered at him. "You're taking me with you or you're not going at all."

"You've got to be kidding me. Get off the fucking car, Madelyn!"

Dexter darted into the back seat without another word. Slade let out a low chuckle but kept out of the conversation.

I kept my gaze focused on my stepbrother, my eyes narrowing. "There's an easy way to get me to move: Say

I can come, and stop acting like such a dick about this whole case. It's not like I *wanted* my car to get stolen."

"Everything after that was your choice," he muttered, glaring at me. "If this is supposed to convince me that you can handle yourself in a difficult situation, it's having the opposite effect."

"Only because that difficult situation is you," I shot back. "If you weren't being such an ass, I wouldn't have needed to resort to tactics like this. And hey, it's working, isn't it?"

"I haven't agreed to anything, and you're not going to force me to give in."

"So intent on running away from your problems." A little acid crept into my voice. *Again*, I could have added.

His own tone turned harsher. "So, you understand that you're the problem here."

I winced inwardly and braced my hands against the smooth metal I was sitting on. "I understand that *you* see me as a problem. I'm sorry it was so inconvenient for me to ask you—a campus organization with your own freaking *office* and everything—for help with something you regularly do as a job."

"None of our other clients sit on the hood of my car and insist on being a part of the investigation," he retorted with an edge that was almost a snarl.

He made a fair point, but I wouldn't let this go. I couldn't. "Somehow I doubt you acted like you couldn't be bothered to take on those clients' cases to begin with either." Or ghosted them for two years after the last time we'd had any significant interaction. "None of them had a reason to believe you might not do your due diligence rather than brushing them off yet again."

"You…" Logan growled.

Before he could follow that up with another insult, Slade's laughter split the air. Both of our heads whipped around.

"Do you have something to say?" Logan spat at him.

Slade shrugged, a glint from the security lamps dancing in his eyes. "She's made a valid point. And she came up with a very effective strategy. I say she's proven that she can handle herself just fine. It's not like we're walking into a murder den. Let her come. The world won't end."

He spoke lightly, but I saw the tension coiled in his stance as he adjusted it. He was trying to defuse our rising tempers—especially Logan's—but he wasn't sure yet if it'd work.

"We don't take civilians on cases with us," Logan said, but his voice wasn't quite as biting as before.

I grimaced at him. "You're not a cop, Logan. You're a student just like me, and we're *both* civilians. Is it the over-inflated ego that has you acting like you're too good to take me with you, or is it something else? Please, I'd love to know."

Logan looked like the top of his head was about to explode with a blast of flame and smoke, but Slade sauntered around the car and gave him a light punch to the arm. "She's spunky. Maybe she'll even be useful at the club. Come on, man."

Club? Before I could ask about that, Logan had run his fingers through his short-cropped hair and then aimed his searing gaze at me again. He pointed his finger in my face, tempting me to slap it away.

"Fine," he said. "You can come along. But the *second* you wimp out of anything or get in the way of the investigation, you're going to back off and give us room to work."

He said it as if he assumed one or the other would happen, and sooner rather than later. Irritation prickled through me, but I raised my chin and slid off the hood without letting it show. I looked forward to proving him wrong.

"I'll take that deal. Now, what's this club we're heading to?"

CHAPTER NINE

Madelyn

We stepped into the dance club on one of the main downtown streets to a staccato house beat, reddish lighting, and a pretty empty dance floor. Almost everyone around at eight pm on a Sunday night was at the bar or one of the small tables set along the walls. I'd heard Keeley mention this place a few times—it was one of the venues she and her friends circulated between for their Friday-night get-togethers—but it obviously wasn't too happening right now.

Which was probably a good thing, since I wasn't sure if the bouncer would have let me in with my basic though fitted jeans and top if there'd been more demand for access.

I came to a stop a few steps inside and glanced at the guys. "There's a chop shop run out of this place?"

Slade guffawed, but he shot me a smile warm enough to smooth over any impression that he was being anything other than good-natured in his teasing. "Right, because with all the car parts lying around, it'd be easy to get confused."

I elbowed him lightly in the ribs as we followed Logan and Dexter toward the bar. I noticed Dexter had taken out his phone, his thumb swiping over it in a careful motion—taking more pictures? "Well, I wouldn't expect them to leave the illegal merchandise out for the regular patrons to see. You did say the chop shops need a cover business."

"It's always someplace that deals more in car-type things," Slade explained. "Mechanics, used vehicle dealers, scrap yards, etc. But we know a few people with ties to the criminal life who come by this place pretty regularly. We'll hit them up for info if they stop by."

Okay, that made a little more sense. I hopped onto a stool at the bar next to Dexter, Slade coming up at my other side and Logan staying on his feet a little farther down. It seemed we were going to try to blend in, since there obviously hadn't been any reason for me *not* to come along. It wasn't as if I was going to push myself into their interrogations. I just wanted to observe.

The woman behind the bar finished splashing and spraying the liquids from various bottles, slid a couple of glasses down the counter to a couple who looked to be in their late twenties, and turned to our group. Her gaze latched on me first. "What can I get you started with?" she asked with a professional but easygoing smile.

"Can I get a mojito with a splash of lemon juice added?" I asked. I rested my hand on my purse, prepared to pull out my fake ID, but she didn't ask. In a college town, she probably figured anyone who looked close to old enough wouldn't come in without supposed proof of their age. The guys were all legal drinking age anyway.

"On it, and for you three?" she asked, shifting her attention to them.

Logan didn't hesitate. "Just a Coke."

"Ginger ale for me," Dexter put in.

"I'll take a Shirley Temple," Slade said with a flirty grin.

Understanding hit me like a jab to the chest, and my cheeks flushed with shamed embarrassment.

Of course. Logan couldn't drink booze without jeopardizing his transplanted liver. The guys must always order non-alcoholic beverages in solidarity. I'd have done the same, but it hadn't really come up when we'd been living at home still in high school. We hadn't gone out to any bars together then, and he wouldn't have been ordering a beer in a restaurant in front of our parents. That factor hadn't even occurred to me in my overall nervous state.

I opened up my purse anyway, feeling the need to do something to show my own commitment to the group. The bartender nudged my drink toward me, and

I pushed enough cash toward her to cover all our orders and a generous tip. "It's all on me."

Logan's head jerked toward me. "You don't have to—"

"I know I don't have to," I said firmly. "But you're helping me out. It's the least I can do."

His mouth flattened, but he didn't say anything else. I doubted he wanted to get into an argument about why we were actually here in front of the other club patrons.

I sipped my cocktail and found it tasted exactly the way I'd wanted, even though I had trouble enjoying it now as I watched the guys grab their less potent drinks. I took a longer gulp, planning to drain the contents quickly so I could switch to a club soda or something.

I couldn't chug it too quickly or the alcohol would rush straight to my head. I still needed to keep my thoughts clear, or I'd prove Logan right about being a liability to the investigation. Taking regular but measured swallows, I studied the rest of the space.

More people were already hitting the dance floor as the night went on. A gaggle of girls bobbed to the beat of the hip hop tune now blaring over the speakers, a few couples and a couple of clusters of single guys dipping and swaying, showing off their moves and laughing together. I felt weirdly isolated sitting here with three men who'd barely wanted me along.

Logan and Dexter appeared to exchange a little conversation, but the music had gotten loud enough that it was difficult to talk. By the time I'd gotten to the bottom of my glass, none of the three had left the bar to approach any other patrons. I frowned and turned to Slade, who seemed like the safest person to ask, even though I had to lean close to avoid shouting obnoxiously over the music. "None of your contacts have shown up yet?"

He shook his head and then tipped it toward Logan, who was just getting up from his stool. My stepbrother made a vague gesture that Slade seemed to understand. When I raised my eyebrows in question, my neighbor flashed another grin. "He's going to scope out the other parts of the club to see if anyone's hiding away in a corner or something."

There was a set of stairs that led to a second floor, I realized. As Logan headed up them and Dexter took another sip of his only half-finished ginger ale, his gaze fixed on the dance floor, Slade slipped off his own stool and sidled even closer to me. "Since we've got no business to take care of yet, we might as well have some fun while we're here. Do you want to dance?"

I blinked at him in surprise before it occurred to me that the invitation was probably all part of blending in. It'd look a bit odd for a few college guys to come into a dance club and not actually do any dancing, especially when they'd brought a girl with them.

Slade confirmed that thought, leaning close enough that I caught the whiff of cinnamon on his breath. "Standing here without dancing looks more suspicious than busting a move on the floor."

I couldn't stop the laugh that escaped me. "Busting a move? What are we, ninety?"

"I promise my dancing will woo you," he teased, extending a hand toward me. "Maybe you'll even take me up on that booty call invitation after this."

Oh, why the hell not? I didn't want to be a stick in the mud or to make us look suspicious. And if Slade wanted to have fun, why shouldn't I?

I pushed off my stool, landing steadily but with a slightly bubbly feeling in my head that told me the mojito's effects had kicked in. Slade snatched my hand and guided me onto the dance floor. As he tugged me around to face him, I started to sway with the music, getting a feel for it. I wasn't a star or anything, but I could hold my own if I needed to.

Slade jumped right into the beat, dipping this way and swiveling that way with a total confidence I couldn't help admiring. I might also have been admiring the physique that justified some of that confidence. The guy was something to look at, and not just because of his moves.

He caught me watching him and waggled his eyebrows before grasping my hand again. "I promised you a real dance. Are you ready for this?"

I bit my bottom lip, unsure of what I'd gotten myself into. "The deal for coming with you was that I didn't wimp out, so show me what you can do."

"I hope you have good balance, Piccolina."

I didn't have a second to question those words before he was sweeping me around, moving me in perfect sync with the music. I barely managed to keep up without stumbling over my own feet. When Slade stopped, he flung my entire body backward. I felt weightless for a moment before he caught me and dipped me close to the floor. Then he lifted me back to his chest in a deft move that left my head spinning.

He slowed his movements for a minute, doing a forward and back move that I could mimic once I found the rhythm. I had to concentrate on each step and motion we made to keep up with what he seemed to be doing flawlessly. Here and there he added little extra gestures that I didn't bother trying to imitate. It looked like a mix of a more formal dance style with typical modern club moves, both coming naturally to him.

Through my awe, I realized I shouldn't be surprised. Back in high school, he'd always liked showing off with agile spins and leaps using his prosthetic leg, proving that it didn't slow him down. It really didn't at all. I mean, he was moving a hell of a lot more gracefully than I was.

He couldn't have come up with all these techniques on his own just goofing around like those teenage antics. As his pace slowed with the more languid beat of the next song, I leaned closer, catching my breath before asking, "Where did you learn to dance like that?"

Slade set his hand on the side of my waist, the contact sending heat flooding through my shirt. It only intensified when he drew me closer so he could speak into my ear. "When I was a kid, my grandfather insisted on teaching me Latin ballroom dancing. He said it would help me win over the ladies when I got older. Is it working?"

I couldn't help snorting at the wry question, giving him a playful shove to the chest, but the truth was, my whole body was getting all kinds of heated up with him this close. "It takes more than a dance to win me over," I informed him with an arch of my eyebrows, but the statement didn't feel all that true.

Slade took the declaration in stride like he did so much else. "Bummer," he said with a wink. The hand on my waist trailed down to my hip, the brush of his fingers making my skin quiver in anticipation. He squeezed lightly, avoiding outright groping my ass, as he wrapped the other arm around the small of my back and dipped me slowly.

I allowed my head to fall back as I laughed through the maneuver. When he raised me, his breath spilled over my upper chest and neck before he pulled me completely upright just inches away from him. I couldn't help imagining what his mouth might have felt like pressed against those sensitive planes.

The thumping beat sped up again, and Slade tugged me even closer to him. His leg eased between my thighs. Suddenly my chest was pressed against his, our bodies swaying together in a way that generated the most delicious friction. It felt incredibly dirty, but I also couldn't bear to stop. It was still just dancing, right?

As much as I tried to convince myself of that, a flush crept over my face. Slade guided me in a rhythmic circle on the dance floor, his lips grazing my cheek. As I let my hands rise to tangle in his wavy hair, he made a sound in the back of his throat that resembled a restrained growl. He whispered a lilting phrase in my ear. "Piccolina, serías el postre perfecto para mi."

My rudimentary Spanish from grade school in no way prepared me to interpret his comment, but it *sounded* good enough to melt me. "What does that mean?" I asked, my voice breathier than intended.

A smirk pulled at his lips as he whirled us in another direction, his leg still rubbing against that hungry spot between my legs. His arm tightened against my back, the muscles flexing. "It means that you would make a delectable dessert."

Okay, it seemed like a simple dance was enough to win me over, after all.

Was *he* really into it, or was this all just passing the time for him? He seemed to flirt automatically, not with any significant intent. I leaned back enough to try to catch his gaze and get a read on him. My heart was pounding fast. I wasn't even sure if I wanted him to be into it. I wasn't actually looking to hook up with him or anything… Right?

The heat I found in Slade's gorgeous eyes was enough to melt any sense of resolve I'd had. A tingle raced through my body to my core. "That—that was a random thought," I murmured, and then could have smacked myself. Of all the things I could have said in response, that was the least sexy option.

Slade didn't seem to mind, though. He licked his lips. "Not as random as you'd think."

His gaze dropped to my mouth, and another rush of heat flooded me. I wanted him to lean in and close the distance between us. I was sure it was a totally horrible idea, but every part of me was aching to find out if he was as good at kissing as he was at dancing.

Oh, hell, Maddie, why not just kiss *him*? The world won't end, right?

I might have actually done it. I hadn't finished arguing with myself when a harsh voice shattered the moment between us.

"Eye-fucking the client on the dance floor—how professional."

Logan's words and his brawny frame looming over us might as well have thrown a bucket of frigid water over me. I pulled away from Slade as if I'd been caught in a crime myself, a shudder running through me.

Slade took a step back too, raising his hands, but he smiled as if he didn't think this was any big deal. "Just fitting in and making use of our time here the way people are supposed to, man."

"Well, while you were getting your rocks off"—Logan's searing gaze snapped to me—"and you were distracting him, I managed to get some information. But there's nothing we can pursue tonight. We should get out of here before we draw any attention—or at least any more than you two might already have."

He sounded even more pissed off than before. If he'd gotten what he wanted to out of this visit, what was his problem? It wasn't like he'd asked Slade to come with him, and I hardly thought we'd made a spectacle of ourselves. Glancing around, none of the other dancers seemed to be paying any attention to us at all—other than a couple who were eyeing *Logan* as if worried he was about to start a brawl.

"The only person making a scene here is you," I informed him.

Logan grimaced at me and whipped around to march back to the bar, where Dexter was still waiting. As he motioned for the other guy to get up from his stool, Slade sauntered close to me again.

"We'll pick this up another time," my dance partner said in a voice laced with promise.

A very large part of me wished we didn't have to wait. What had he been planning on doing next?

Of course freaking Logan just *had* to interrupt at the worst possible moment—and with his continuing hostility that I didn't really understand at all. If anyone should be pissed off at anyone here, it was me at *him*.

But as much as he was acting like an ass, I needed to behave at least enough to ensure I'd get to come along on whatever the next steps of the investigation were. Dragging in a breath to even out my temper, I strode over to join the guys on the way out the door.

What exactly had Logan found out anyway?

CHAPTER
TEN

Beckett

The girl moved briskly through the grocery store —I lost track of her here and there in the aisles from my vantage point outside the large front windows. She wasn't particularly noticeable anyway—a typical college student with straight blond hair that hung down her back and a slim frame. Pretty, sure, but not startlingly so.

The only reason I'd noticed her in the club last night was the company she'd been keeping. Those three guys had been poking their noses into a lot of places they really didn't belong. I wasn't sure what their end game was. Often a girlfriend was the weakest link, the easiest way to get my questions answered without my actual targets having a clue.

I tapped absently at my phone, pretending I was actually texting someone on it and just casually glancing up while I waited for responses. The girl grabbed a couple of sodas off a shelf and vanished from view again. None of her purchases had been remarkable either.

I wasn't going to learn much from watching. I needed to make an approach—one that would ensure a longer interaction, endear me to her, and offer the opportunity to earn some trust upfront. How I handled it would depend on where she went next.

My phone vibrated faintly with an actual incoming text. I diverted my attention briefly to check its contents.

It was from Lana, the woman who handled a lot of the day-to-day administrative work for my family's business. *There was a bit of a squabble with a group in Atlanta over their tariff. How do you want to handle it?*

I bit back a sigh. There were always minor players trying to buck the system. It never worked out well for them.

Email me the details, I wrote back. *And let them know they have until tomorrow to make things right, or we'll right things for them.*

Understood.

Technically, she should have been asking my dad. Because technically, Dad was still in charge of our family's empire. But Lana knew as well as I did that she'd get a faster answer—and a better one—from me these days.

That was why I had to be especially wary of random upstarts interfering with any of our business ventures.

When I glanced up again, the blond girl was at the checkout counter. She slung her two bags over her arms and headed for the door. I eased off to the side, examining my phone again but tracking her from the corner of my eye.

She considered the street and walked with a peppy stride toward the coffee shop on the corner. A perfect opportunity. I started meandering after her, much more slowly, pausing for more pretend text-tapping once she'd darted inside.

Through the slightly grimy window of the mom-and-pop place a lot of the college students favored, I followed her progress from cash register to order pick-up counter, where she grabbed a predictable iced latte, and then on toward the door again. That was my cue.

I tugged at my shirt sleeves instinctively, my fingers brushing the simple but elegant cufflinks that'd been a fourteenth birthday gift from Dad. Back when he'd paid more attention to matters of business, he'd instilled in me the belief that you should look as well put-together as you kept your affairs. That was what made people respect you before they even knew you. Not that my clothes were going to matter that much in a few seconds anyway, but I'd make the most of them all the same.

I ambled onward, angling myself so I'd pass within a foot of the coffee shop doorway. I stepped in front if it just as the girl hustled outside, juggling her bags of groceries and the cup of iced coffee that was filled to the brim.

She gave a little yelp as our arms collided. I twisted

as if to try to get out of the way, but managed to ensure that some of her coffee spurted out of the lid to splash across my button-up. Then I jerked backward as if startled, staring down at the light brown blotch spreading across the ivory fabric.

"Oh, crap, crap, crap," the girl muttered, shoving herself out of the way of the entrance and setting her coffee on a nearby bench. Her voice was lower than I'd expected, serious and a little husky—not the high-pitched cheerleader squeal I'd imagined. "I'm so sorry."

I shook my head with a bemused chuckle and grabbed a tissue from my pocket to dab at the stain. "Damn. Well, it's just a shirt. And it's my fault too. I should have been watching where I was going." I shot her a smile, just a little bit of teeth, warm but not overdoing it. "I should apologize to you for stealing some of your coffee."

She blinked at me and then seemed to struggle to hold back a laugh. She failed, a soft guffaw spilling out. "Don't be silly. I'm the one who ruined *your* shirt. I can —I'll give you some money to cover the cleaning costs."

I waved her off, still smiling. "Really, don't worry about it. I'll be able to get it out in the wash." The lie slipped effortlessly from my lips. Even dry cleaning might not remove the stain; the shirt was probably a loss. But it was a minor sacrifice. "Don't worry, I'm not one of those guys who doesn't have a clue how to do his own laundry."

"Oh, I wasn't trying to imply that." She bit her lip, and it occurred to me that close up she was more appealing than I'd first given her credit for. Or maybe that was less about the details of her face and more the fact that she obviously wasn't at all ditzy. Her concern felt totally genuine. "I still feel bad. Are you sure there isn't anything I can do to make up for it?"

And so generous with that opening. I let my smile stretch a little wider and tipped my head toward her bags. "Clearly the problem is that you're carrying too much. How about you let me help you with your bags so I can ensure no one else's shirt meets the same fate mine did?"

Her eyes narrowed slightly—she was smart enough to be wary of a random stranger offering to carry her things. But I'd phrased it in such a way that it didn't sound like too much of a come-on, and it wasn't as if her snacks were all that valuable. And I could tell she was a little intrigued by me.

"That sounds like *you'd* be doing *me* a favor," she said, shifting her weight.

I shrugged. "I'd see it more as a favor to humanity in general. I'm guessing you're heading to the college campus? I have to walk that way anyway to get back to my car. You might as well be able to enjoy the rest of your coffee without having to do a juggling act."

Her eyebrow arched a smidge, but she handed over one of the bags. She paused for a moment afterward as if confirming I wasn't going to run off with it or something, but it must have been obvious this would have been a very strange scam. If that were the scam I was running.

"I am going back to campus," she said as we moved to cross the street. "Is it that obvious?"

I glanced down at her bag. "These totally look like study snacks. And this is the part of the city where most of the students come to shop. Just an educated guess. Have you been at the university for long? I haven't seen you around before."

She laughed again, a little more relaxed this time. "I don't leave the campus all that often. My roommate says I study too much. And I only transferred here a few months ago."

"I hear it's a good university," I said. Always good to lead with reasonably innocuous but friendly small talk. "I'm glad you got in. I'm Beckett, by the way."

"Madelyn," the girl said automatically, and then clamped her mouth as if she was thinking better of having given her name that freely. "I guess *you're* not a student," she ventured after a moment.

I'd already given that away with my comment about having simply heard the university was good. At twenty-three, I could have claimed to be a grad-student, but there was no point in lying about things so easily exposed.

I didn't have to be specific about the truth either, though. She might not be a typical college girl, but I doubted she'd have a high opinion of the ways I'd gotten the most important parts of my education.

"Not at the moment," I said. "My school days are behind me. What are you studying, Madelyn?"

"Biology. Maybe a second major in microbiology if

the classes line up with my schedule, but I'm not sure about that yet."

She rattled off those facts so easily that I could let out an impressed whistle without needing to fake my reaction at all. She was definitely a smarter cookie than I'd have given her credit for at a glance. Not just a science major, but considering a double major? I might not have ever attended university here, but I knew the place had a reputation for its science program. She'd have needed excellent grades to get in, and it'd be a challenging program to keep up with.

Maybe she wasn't going to be the weak link I'd needed after all.

But school smarts were a very different thing from street smarts, as I should know. "You must be awfully busy," I said. "I can see why you'd need to spend a lot of time studying. It mustn't leave much room for enjoying the rest of the college experience."

"Oh, I get out enough to stop me from going bonkers. I've never been a party animal anyway."

I could easily believe that now. "Fair enough. I was just thinking, it must be hard to even socialize much— keeping up with friends, relationships."

"To be honest, I don't have a whole lot of those," Madelyn said with another laugh, this one slightly embarrassed.

I cocked an eyebrow at her. "Oh, no? Pretty girl like you?" Then I knit my brow as if I'd just remembered something. "You know, I think I have seen you in town before, from a distance, with some guy... Dark hair, maybe Latino? That's probably why I assumed. It might not have been you at all."

The guy she'd been dancing with at the club had certainly *looked* like he wanted to get a whole lot more than friendly with her. He'd been a few beats from fucking her right there on the dance floor, as far as I'd been able to tell. Maybe it'd just been a fling, but Madelyn wasn't striking me as the kind of girl who went for friends-with-benefits or one-night stands.

"Oh," she said, and her cheeks flushed a deeper pink that told me the interest between the two of them wasn't all on his side.

The sight brought an unexpected flare of annoyance into my chest. I should have wanted her to be invested in the trio so that she'd have information to share, but some part of me wanted to growl at the thought of him putting his hands on her again.

"The only guys I've gone anywhere with recently are just friends," she went on. "Well, maybe only acquaintances—I don't know how to label them exactly..." She trailed off, looking even more flustered. Interesting, even though it provoked another jab of jealousy.

"Sounds a bit complicated," I said in a gently teasing tone meant to set her back at ease, and then added more seriously, "I hope they're not jerking you around."

"Oh, no, nothing like that," she said, a bit too quickly I thought. "They just—they're helping me with a sort of project, that's all. We've only met up a couple of times."

There was more to it than she was saying, I could tell. I couldn't discern whether she was involved with them enough that she'd know anything about the activities I was curious about, though.

But maybe it didn't matter, because the more I'd talked to her, the more she'd intrigued *me*. A biology major who didn't socialize much but was perfectly gracious when I'd gotten her into a jam, who'd somehow gotten entangled with three guys who were delving into the city's criminal underworld?

I had the feeling there was so much more to her than I'd uncovered yet. But we'd just reached the edge of campus. She stopped and turned to me, and my heart sank more than I was prepared for, especially as I took in her apologetic smile that nonetheless brightened her pretty face.

"Well, this is me. Thank you for your help with the bag, and sorry again about your shirt. I promise I'm not usually that clumsy."

I doubted she was, not when she wasn't being set up. I handed the bag over to alleviate any worries she might have had that I was going to draw out the conversation by holding her belongings hostage.

Should I ask for her phone number? No, she'd probably find that too forward. I was still essentially a stranger to her, and she obviously wasn't the type to collect potential boyfriends. Anyway, I didn't want her mentioning anything about me to her friends—maybe acquaintances, maybe something more—which meant keeping this meeting low key.

"It was my pleasure," I said smoothly. "And I swear the spill was no big deal. I hope I'll see you around again, Madelyn. In the meantime, good luck with your studies."

Her shoulders relaxed when I didn't push for anything else, and I knew I'd made the right call. "Thanks, Beckett. Maybe we will run into each other again."

She gave a little wave with the hand holding her now-half-empty coffee cup and walked off toward the university buildings. I watched her for a few seconds, admiring the resoluteness in her stride that I hadn't registered before, and then strolled away.

Oh, she would be seeing me again. Before very long, too. I didn't need her phone number to ensure that. I could arrange another 'coincidental' meet-up as easy as snapping my fingers.

It was only a matter of time until I found out what I needed—and satisfied all my newfound curiosity about *her* too.

CHAPTER
ELEVEN

Madelyn

"They actually brought you along?" Summer said, her thin eyebrows rising on my phone's screen. "I thought Logan was trying to keep you out of the investigation."

I bit into one of the cookies I'd gotten from the grocery store this morning as I considered my answer. Naturally my best friend had asked about my stolen car investigation not long after we'd started this video chat, and naturally I'd told her about last night's excursion, but I wasn't sure I was going to like her response to the full story.

I squirmed on my dorm-room bed and made myself look directly at the phone where it was propped on my pillow. The chewy sweetness of the oatmeal chocolate chip cookie only offset my uneasiness a little. "Well... he didn't *want* to bring me. I basically sat on the hood of his car until he gave in, and he swore that as soon as I messed up, which he assumes I'll do, he's never letting me get involved again. But he did let me come. And I didn't mess anything up. So there."

Summer lowered her fork from where she'd been bringing a bite of her lunch to her mouth. Her round face with its high cheekbones looked most natural when it was full of energy, either playful or determined. I didn't like the somberness that darkened it now.

"Maddie, he argued with you about it until you forced his hand? Just to tag along to a club that regular people go to all the time? He's still *such* an asshole."

I winced. "I know. I realize he's being an asshole. But the three of them seem to know what they're doing as far as tracking down clues. I can put up with Logan's crap for a little while if it means I get my stuff back."

Summer sighed and swept her long, smooth hair behind her ear. She'd dyed the dark strands with henna so they had a burgundy tint now. "Come on. I know you. You're not just insisting on going along because it's your car. Don't tell me you're not still hoping you'll get answers out of him."

"He didn't *use* to be an asshole," I burst out, and flushed when I realized how I'd raised my voice. "Something's going on with him," I added in a more subdued tone. "Something's been going on with him for a while. If I can find out what, then that wouldn't be a bad thing. But I'm not, like, pining over him or something, Summer. I'm *way* over that."

"I don't know. Sometimes people just change."

Summer grimaced. "Look, I can admit that he wasn't a bad guy before. I remember him in high school—I know he stood up for you back in junior high. Maybe that guy is still in there underneath, but I hope you're prepared that he could simply be an asshole all the way through. Because he's had more than enough time to get his head out of his ass by now."

My shoulders slumped. I had no argument against the points she'd made. "I'm not expecting anything. Mostly I just want to find my car and my dad's box."

Summer offered me a small but warm smile that brought more of the usual glow back to her face. "I don't mean to get on your case about it. I just hated seeing what he did to you, and I don't want him hurting you again. That's all."

"Believe me," I said, "I'm not going to let him in enough that he could hurt me again. I know better than that."

"Of course you do." Summer's smile stretched into a grin. "You're Madelyn Silver, lady conqueror."

I snorted. "I haven't conquered much other than cookies and lab reports lately, but I'm working on it."

Summer's gaze flicked to the side. "Crap, I've got to get going for my next class. Talk soon?"

"Always."

After we'd ended the call, restlessness wound through my bones. I hadn't received any updates from the Vigil so far today. Had they gotten anywhere with the info Logan had pried out of whoever he'd talked to at the club—info he'd refused to share with me because he'd claimed he didn't want me going off on my own to dig into it. Like he cared about my safety and not just acting like some kind of professional detective.

I could go over to the Vigil office and find out. The guys seemed to hang out there a lot—it also made a perfect study spot while they were on campus, after all. Hopefully I'd catch one of them. If not, I'd swing by again after my afternoon class.

I hopped off the bed and grabbed my backpack and a thin hoodie in case the early spring air cooled again later in the day. When I stepped out of the building, the breeze swept over me with a subtle warmth that loosened some of the tension in my shoulders. The scent of freshly mowed grass tickled my nose, a smell that always made me feel like spring had really arrived. I sucked in a deep breath and strode forward.

Maybe some of my high school crusades had been a little over the top, but Summer was right. I could conquer anything I put my mind to.

I was just coming up on the law library, about ten feet from the front door, when a tall, brawny figure ducked through the doorway and headed along the side of the building toward a different path. Logan. He looked so lost in thought I didn't know if he'd even noticed me.

My feet stalled for a second as my pulse hiccupped. Then I pushed myself forward, hurrying after him.

Who knew when I'd have the chance to talk to him alone again? Summer was right that it was well past time that I got some answers. How ridiculous had it been when I'd been chatting with that guy Beckett this morning and I stumbled all over explaining who my stepbrother and his friends were to me?

I'd shied away from addressing the real problems between us, but that wasn't the kind of woman I was. I wasn't going to let him turn me into a cringing wimp just because he'd tossed me away like a dirty tissue two years ago.

"Logan!" I said as I closed the distance between us, holding on to the surge of boldness that'd propelled me after him.

I couldn't help noticing the way he stiffened at the sound of my voice, which he'd no doubt recognized. He wasn't happy to hear me calling after him at all. Well, tough cookies, Mr. Brooks.

I half expected him to march onward pretending he hadn't heard me, but he spun on his heel to face me, his expression hard.

I came to a stop in front of him, tucking my thumbs around the straps of my backpack as if for leverage. "We need to talk."

"I actually have somewhere to be," he said curtly.

I shrugged. "Fine. Then I'll walk with you and we'll talk on the way to wherever you're going."

Logan's mouth flattened, which told me he didn't really have anywhere all that urgent he needed to go. "What's so important, Madelyn? We don't know anything else about your car yet, but of course you could have just texted about that."

Well, he'd just given me the perfect opening. I

folded my arms over my chest. "That'd be a little hard considering you have me blocked on every form of communication I'm aware of."

A muscle in his jaw twitched. Oh, was this topic of conversation irritating to him? Too fucking bad.

"You have the other guys' numbers," he said. "You don't need mine."

I stared him down, drawing my spine as straight as I could. "But I do need to know what the hell happened with us?"

"With us?" A hint of a sneer crept into his voice. "There's no 'us,' and there never was."

My teeth set on edge. He got under my skin way too easily.

"We were friends," I said. "Or at least friendly. We got along in school and after our parents started dating, for years. And then all of a sudden you just put all these walls up. And then there was—two years ago—and then you *completely* shut me out like I'd done something awful to you… And you're still treating me like that. I don't get it. Why are you being like this? Why *have* you been like this?"

My voice was raw by the end of that tirade. I hadn't meant to say so much all at once, but once I'd started, it'd kept spilling out. I clamped my jaw shut and held Logan's gaze, daring him to finally give me a straight answer.

But of course that was wishful thinking.

"Not everything in the world revolves around you," he said, his voice getting even terser. "And you don't have the right to know everything that's going on in my life just because our parents got married."

Fury blazed through me at the brisk dismissal. "Oh, yeah? And what about what happened in the basement bathroom back home? Do I have a right to know about *that*, considering I was there and all?"

"All that happened was a stupid mistake," Logan bit out, the words hitting me like little knives. "I moved on. It's obviously time that you did too."

Something in me crumbled even as I held myself steady on the outside. *A stupid mistake.* Was that how he thought about it?

"I just don't get it," I said, quieter now. "If you have some problem with me or with something I did, you could just tell me about it. We used to talk. I thought you liked me, as a person. It seemed totally out of the blue. And then— Something must have happened, Logan."

He shook his head, his eyes flashing, his shoulders rigid. "You only see what you want to see. And you obviously can't take a hint. I'm not into you. I don't want anything to do with you. I can't wait until we find your car and we can go our separate ways again. But you *had* to follow me all the way to the same college… Do you have any idea how pathetic that is?"

I flinched as if he'd slapped me. It felt like he had. Was that really what he thought of me? That I was some clueless girl who'd transferred over a hopeless crush?

"I didn't come here because of you," I shot back, my hands clenching as they dropped to my sides. "This school has an amazing life sciences program, way better than the college back home, and—"

"And a dozen other schools in this part of the country have good programs too. If you had the grades to get in here, you could have gone anywhere else in the country too. But no, you had to come to the same school as me."

"I liked not being too far from home." My voice wobbled, my emotions fraying both in the wake of his hostility and because I knew he wasn't totally wrong. I'd come here for the science program first, but the fact that it'd meant I might see Logan again, might find out what was going on with him, had been there in the back of my mind. I hadn't really considered applying anywhere else.

Logan ignored my protest. He jabbed a finger in my direction. "You're nothing to me except a temporary client, and you can forget about becoming anything more than that. So get over yourself and find someone else to obsess over."

He whipped around and stalked off without giving me a chance to say anything else. Not that I had any idea what I could have said. My throat had constricted so tightly it ached.

I still couldn't wrap my head around how he'd gone from my defender and friend to a guy who seemed to hate me. It was *because* of him that I'd become the crusader Summer had referred to me as. I'd been so downcast after Dad's death that I'd become an increasingly easy target for the kind of kids who liked to poke fun and pull cruel pranks, and I hadn't snapped out of that haze until I'd watched Logan put those bullies in their place on my behalf.

Hearing him talk them into submission, leveraging his popularity to my advantage, had made me want to be stronger. To be able to stand up not just for myself but for other people who needed it, like Logan had for me. That was what Dad would have wanted too—not for me to end up withdrawn and eaten up by guilt.

But somewhere in the last few years, something had changed. Logan clearly wasn't interested in telling me what. Maybe there really wasn't any reason to do with me at all. Maybe he had simply changed into a total asshole.

I swallowed thickly and gave myself a shake, pulling myself together. Whatever. It didn't change anything—I'd never thought we'd actually become friends again, let alone anything more. I could live without an explanation.

But it did tell me that no way in hell did I trust him to keep me in the loop about the investigation. Had they really not made any progress, or was he lying about that so he could shut me out there too?

I walked back to the law library, gathering confidence as I left the conversation behind. Screw Logan, and screw his fucked-up attitude. He thought he could go around doing whatever and treating people however he wanted? I could take a page out of that book.

I brushed past the main desk and hustled onward to

the Vigil's office at the back of the room. The doorknob turned with a twist. I peeked inside, a little surprised that it'd actually worked, and found Dexter sitting at the computer, typing away. He paused to glance over at me, his eyes catching mine for just a second before veering away. "Hi, Madelyn. Did something come up about your car?"

I guessed there really wasn't anything new if he'd ask me that instead of assuming I'd come to him for information. But a strange calm settled over me as I looked back at him. Dexter had given me straight answers so far. He didn't try to push my buttons like either of the other guys in their very different ways.

Between the three of them, he was the only member of the Vigil I trusted to treat me fairly and to put the investigation and my stake in it first.

I walked over until I was a few feet from his seat. I stopped there, biting my lip. "No news on my end. But... do you think you could do me a small favor?"

CHAPTER
TWELVE

Slade

pushed harder through the last two reps of my workout, making my body strain to keep up, and I finished with sweat beading across my forehead and down my back. The campus gym had an expensive setup with plenty of room for students, and I took full advantage. All three of us did, even if Dexter was a little more infrequent in his visits. We knew that strength and flexibility might be the difference between life and death one day with the kind of shit we got into.

I grabbed the spray bottle and wiped down the bench and the weights that I'd been pressing, followed by a swipe of my face with the front of my muscle tee. The burn spreading through my muscles told me I'd made good use of my time.

I headed over to the rooms where the more structured fitness activities were held. Logan's kickboxing session should be just finishing up. Just as I reached the short hallway, he came around the corner, equally sweaty but looking just as grim as when we'd come in.

Damn. I'd been hoping he'd work some of that bad temper out of him. No such luck.

He nodded to me, and we walked together to the locker room.

"Good class?" I asked.

Logan grunted. "I took down everyone I was up against except one jerk who kept trying to skirt the rules."

"Hmm. I guess we're not much of anyone to complain about that approach."

Logan grimaced at me and grabbed the locker room door, holding it open so I could pass in front of him. If anyone else had done that, I might have been irritated, but I knew from him it wasn't a sign that he was catering to some assumed feebleness. He'd have done the same for Dexter, just automatically. Logan always felt like he had to do a little more of the heavy lifting.

"It was a good workout, anyway," he said as we headed toward the shower stalls. A couple of guys passing us glanced down at the bright blue prosthetic poking from beneath my shorts with widening eyes, and then hustled on by when I gave them a wave and a cheery grin. I snorted and refocused on my best friend.

He did look a little looser than when we'd come in. Maybe I could get away with some of the prying I'd been wanting to do ever since the club a couple of nights ago.

I grabbed my towel, soap, and disinfectant wipes and marched toward the shower stall at the end of the row that had a bar on the wall for extra support. Logan followed, taking the one beside mine as I bent over and unstrapped the prosthetic from the stump that served as my knee. After all that sweating, I'd take extra care to disinfect it after showering.

I propped the prosthetic on the bench outside the shower where I could still see it from the stall and hopped inside with a hand on the bar. I might prefer to make use of the same facilities as everyone else when I could match them just fine, but I could admit that in certain situations I needed a little extra help. Wet floors on one foot were a recipe for disaster. As I'd unfortunately found out back in my elementary school days in an incident I'd had to work very hard to erase from my classmates' memories with a whole lot of other antics.

I tossed my clothes onto the bench from the stall and turned on the water. After I'd given my hair a quick scrub, I angled my head out of the water enough that I could talk.

"You seem like you had a lot of stress to work off," I said casually. "Anything in particular on your mind? I'm trying to avoid thinking about the end-of-term essay that's been kicking my ass."

Logan made a dismissive sound. "It's always good to blow off some energy."

I leaned into the shower wall as I poured a generous amount of body wash in my hands and began smearing it across my body. "Does that energy have a name? Maybe Madelyn Silver?"

Logan took a long moment to reply, and my smile only grew. "It has nothing to do with her," he muttered.

I guffawed. "Yeah? I thought you were a *good* liar. So there's been something between you, huh?"

"Yeah, right. Her fucking case is frustrating as hell. Having her insert herself into the middle of it isn't any picnic either. That's all."

Why was he lying to me about it, even after I'd prodded him? *Was* he lying? Thinking back to the way he'd looked when he'd broken up our dance in the club, how pissed off he'd been, I didn't think I'd imagined the flash of jealousy in his eyes. There hadn't been any other reason for him to be pissed off. He'd gotten to talk to his contact. Nothing had gone wrong.

Of course, considering how wrapped up *I'd* gotten in Maddie's charms in that moment, maybe I'd been interpreting his reaction through that lens. He could have simply been irritated that I was getting involved with her in ways beyond the case, since he was so intent on shutting her out of our lives as quickly as possible.

"Seriously?" I wheedled. "You got to live in the same house as a girl that hot and you never even played a little tonsil hockey?"

"Get your mind out of the gutter for once, Slade. I wasn't exactly so short on options I needed to go after my own stepsister. She's a major annoyance, and that's it."

His tone firmed with the last words in a way that said, *End of conversation.*

I rinsed myself off quickly and gave my body a swift rub-down with my towel before hefting myself out of the stall to sink onto the bench. As I tugged on my clothes, Logan emerged, getting himself together with equal briskness. He didn't seem interested in continuing any kind of conversation with me at all now.

As I slipped the sock over my stump, my mind drifted back to Maddie. I'd *tried* to follow the bro code and determine his feelings for her. If he was going to insist she was nothing but an irritation to him, then what could I do but take him at face value? I'd given him every opportunity to inform me that he had a stake there or that my presumably obvious interest bothered him, and he hadn't said a word.

If he lost a chance he wouldn't even admit he wanted to take because I got there first, then it'd be his own damn fault.

Because lord, did I want to go there. I'd already been impressed by the way Maddie had stood up to Logan. Not many people were willing to challenge him as openly as she had on multiple occasions in just the past few days. And then dancing with her, feeling her rise to *that* challenge even though the steps hadn't been familiar to her, doing her best to match me…

She might not have quite kept up with the actual moves, but she'd given herself over to the rhythm rather than stiffening up. She'd trusted me to guide her. And the feel of that sleekly curvy body against mine…

From the little I'd known of her back in high school, I'd never have expected to find her this attractive. She'd been pretty, sure, but she'd also been the studious type, only stepping into the spotlight when she was taking on one cause or another. I'd had no idea that passion permeated so many other parts of her life. What would it be like to soak it up in every possible way?

To move my hands over those curves without clothes between us. To claim those pouty lips. To hear the sounds she'd make as I unraveled her. To find out just how well *she* could unravel me.

Fuck. Just thinking about it was getting me hard, like I was a preteen who'd just caught a glimpse of a hot girl's cleavage and not a grown man who should have better self-control. She had an effect on me, all right.

And she was so much more than just a body. There was that boldness that drew me to her, but she had a caring streak a mile wide to go along with it. She barely knew me, and I was best friends with the guy who was giving her the hardest time in the history of the universe right now, but she'd still offered to use her contacts to see if I could try out one of those experimental prosthetics.

If she'd had any idea how much we weren't telling her—how much *I* wasn't telling her…

A knot of guilt twisted my stomach. I glanced over at Logan as I reattached my prosthetic. "Are we really going to keep Maddie in the dark about the bigger picture? I mean, now that she's kind of crashed our party already."

Logan's eyes hardened. "Are you kidding me? She's already pushing her way into places she doesn't belong just over her car. Nothing good would come from getting her involved in the rest."

His voice was firm, but I couldn't help pushing a little harder. "Is anything good going to come out of hiding it from her?"

Logan spun on me, his eyes flashing, and loomed with the few inches he had over me in a way I'd normally only seen him use on perps we were intimidating. "No one should say anything to Madelyn about *any* of our work other than her stolen car. Or do you have a problem with that?"

There was an understated threat in his voice. I swallowed hard, abruptly ashamed of provoking him. I knew what a sensitive subject it was, and he knew more about that area of our investigations than Dexter or I did. As much as we'd all worked on it together, it was his pet project. He should know what could get us into more danger.

"No, man, of course not," I said. "If you say that's a no go, then it's a no go. I just thought it was worth asking."

Logan held my gaze for a few seconds longer before his stance relaxed. As he turned to tuck the rest of his belongings into his bag, I adjusted the sock over my stump to make sure it wasn't creased in an uncomfortable way against the prosthetic. It'd taken me a while to adjust when I was a little kid, but for most of my life, wearing the thing had been as normal as putting on a pair of sneakers was for anyone else.

We headed out together, and I groped for another topic of conversation. Something that had nothing to do with Madelyn or anything else that might piss my best friend off. But as we stepped out of the building, Logan's phone dinged with an incoming text.

He pulled it out of his pocket and paused in mid-stride. Then he shot me a tight smile. "The guy I talked to at the club came through. We've got a new lead to check out—and we should get on it fast."

CHAPTER
THIRTEEN

Madelyn

stepped out of the Uber and glanced at the concrete-walled building across the street, which had a rack of tires out front. A large neon sign above the entrance read, "Javier's Mechanic Shop," and below it, in smaller writing, was what appeared to be a list of the most common services. Contrasting with the old, yellowing color of the concrete, Logan's dark sedan was parked off to the side. All three of the Vigil members stood around it, heads bent together as if they were discussing their approach to the situation at hand.

I checked the traffic and hustled across the road before striding toward them. Slade noticed me first, confusion and then amusement flickering through his expression. Dexter's eyes pierced into mine next, revealing nothing of his thoughts before he looked back at Logan. My stepbrother finally glanced over his shoulder.

His gaze collided with mine. It didn't surprise me when his lips tightened and his expression hardened, but his reaction to my presence still stung. I could only imagine what he was thinking, remembering the way he'd blatantly told me to take a hint only to find me in front of him without his invitation.

"What are you doing here?" he demanded, turning to fully face me.

"Helping find my car." I shrugged, stopping a few feet away from them and crossing my arms. "The same thing that I told you I was going to do from the start."

Logan's jaw worked. "How did you even know we'd be here?"

Frustration flared in my chest. "Oh, you mean because you didn't fill me in, even though you said I could be part of the investigation as long as I didn't screw things up? I was really hoping that you would have kept your word, but I wasn't going to put too much stake in that, so I asked Dexter to text me if you came up with any leads."

Logan's gaze shot to Dexter, his eyes narrowing, before refocusing on me. "You went behind my back?"

My laugh came out harsh. "Only because you went behind mine. I asked him to keep me up to date on the investigation since I apparently can't trust you to do that. Dexter, at least, is good to his word."

"This isn't a part that you should be around for. That's the only reason I didn't tell you."

I snorted. "It's pretty clear you don't think I should be around for any of it, so forgive me if I'm not going to go by your word on that. At this point, I couldn't give a rat's ass how you feel. You gave me your word that I could help, so I'm going to help. It's as simple as that."

And I just wouldn't think about all the other things he'd said since then.

Logan swung around to glare at Dexter. "And you see no problem with tipping her off without my go-ahead?"

Dexter held his gaze for a moment before his focus veered elsewhere, but he stayed totally calm, no sign that he was intimidated by the bigger guy. "She hasn't interfered with anything we've been doing yet. We did agree to let her join in as long as she didn't get in the way."

Slade chuckled and popped one of his cinnamon candies into his mouth. "You never told us specifically that we *shouldn't* talk to Maddie about it, Logan. Dexter went by what you said rather than what you didn't. If you didn't want her here, you shouldn't have made the deal."

The support from the other two guys gave me the confidence to raise my chin and glower at Logan. "I'm only sticking around until I get my stuff back. Don't worry, I won't be a *pathetic* shadow once this is all over."

Something flashed in Logan's eyes, but he was the one who looked away first. His shoulders rigid, he stalked into the mechanic shop without another word. I didn't think going in there furious was going to help him handle the situation right, but who was I to tell *him* what to do? If he ruined things, he'd have no one to blame but himself.

Slade motioned to me as he and Dexter moved to follow. "Stay close to us and take a good look around. Let us know if you see any sign of your car—or parts that could have come from it. Otherwise, it's better if you focus on watching rather than talking—we've got more experience with guys like these."

He said it smoothly without a hint that he was being patronizing, which made the instructions a lot easier to swallow than if they'd come in the tone Logan usually took with me. I nodded and hustled after him. The last thing I wanted to do was make a misstep and prove my infuriating stepbrother right.

It appeared Logan had gotten his own frustrations in check quickly. I found him approaching the reception desk with a confident but unruffled air.

"I need to check on a car I brought in," he said to the man behind the desk.

The guy squinted at him and then tapped at his computer, looking a bit puzzled.

I scanned the front office quickly. It was clean enough, the linoleum floor a bit scuffed around the edges of the industrial rug. A few pictures of men standing in front of retro cars hung on the walls. Nothing appeared particularly suspicious to my inexperienced eyes or related to my missing vehicle.

"And your name is…?" the guy at the desk said to Logan, but Slade was ambling past the desk to a door across from it. He was already pushing it open when the guy gave a shout. "Hey, clients don't go in the bay!"

But Slade had sauntered right into the gloomier space I vaguely made out beyond the doorway, acting like he owned the place, and as the guy from the desk hurried over, Logan and Dexter followed. I darted after them, remembering Slade's warning to stick with them.

"Just want to make sure the work's being done right," Slade was saying breezily. He and the other guys fanned out in different directions through the large bay that held a couple of cars on jacks as well as one right on the stained cement floor. Dexter had taken out his phone, no doubt snapping pictures of everything around us, but none of the three cars looked anything like mine.

I followed him instinctively, since he was the one who'd let me tag along to begin with. The guy from the desk hesitated in the doorway as the phone rang behind him. "You need to get out of here," he snapped at the Vigil guys before dashing back to answer it.

A man in a grease-smudged undershirt and jeans scrambled out from under the car he'd been working on. He swiped his hands on his pants and started toward Logan. "What the hell are you kids doing in here? This is employees only."

How long were we going to manage to stay in this part of the shop? I forced my gaze to skim across the room, taking in all the details I could absorb.

Unfortunately, I didn't know much about cars. I could tell none of the three in front of me were mine, but what about that stack of parts in the corner? Had any of them come from my ride? Was there anything suspicious about the racks of tools along the back wall? Did chop shops use equipment a regular mechanic didn't?

Okay, so I was a little out of my depth. But I did know *my* car better than any of the guys here. That had to count for something.

Logan turned toward the advancing mechanic without any sign of concern. "We're looking for a 2006 Chevy Malibu," he said casually. "Green. Have you had one brought in recently?"

A slight edge had crept into his voice, and he folded his arms over his chest, the substantial muscles there flexing. Even I could read the understated threat that he wasn't going to be happy if the workers lied to him about it.

"You see a Malibu around here?" the mechanic demanded, waving his hand toward the rest of the bay.

"Maybe it's in bits and pieces now," Logan suggested, striding onward. The other guys moved deeper into the bay, checking out every inch of the space, so I drifted after them, my heart thumping fast.

The mechanic stomped toward them. "Get the fuck out of here!"

"Or what?" Slade drawled. "You'll call the police on us? I'm sure you *really* want the cops poking around here."

I didn't know if he'd seen something to confirm that statement or was just acting on instinct, but the mechanic stiffened a bit. His face flushed with anger. I braced myself for what he'd do next—and didn't register the rasp of footsteps behind me before it was too late.

Thick arms swung around me from behind, pinning my elbows to my sides. The smell of stale sweat washed over me as a broad body yanked me against him with a menacing guffaw. His voice came out hoarsely hostile. "Maybe they'll listen when they know their girl will get hurt if they don't."

For the first instant, my body froze up. But then years of self-defense training kicked in. The Krav Maga philosophy that we'd been reminded of nearly every class flashed through my mind: when facing a potential threat, react as quickly as possible and with all the force necessary to get yourself out of the danger.

I jerked my elbows wide, hard enough to force my attacker's grip to slide up my arms in his surprise. When he tried to tighten his hold, I jerked to the side, clenched my hand into a fist, and slammed it backward one, two, three times into his groin.

The first blow glanced off his thigh, but the second and third landed. The guy groaned and stumbled backward, and I broke from his hold, swinging around to shove him even farther away. My other hand whipped across his face, smacking into his nose just before my heel rammed into his gut.

The last move nearly screwed me over. I didn't retract my leg quite fast enough, and the big guy managed to snatch my ankle while he clutched his groin with his other hand. He yanked, and I staggered, losing my balance. I tried to catch the back of a nearby car, but my forearm just scraped across the edge of its bumper. Pain seared through my arm.

As I hit the floor ass first, my attacker sprang at me, but I wasn't cowed. I kicked out again and managed to jab the full force of my foot right between his legs where he was already tender.

"Fuck!" he shouted, crumpling with one hand pressed to his junk again and the other to his nose, which was dribbling blood from my previous blow.

I scrambled backward on the floor, vaguely aware of the Vigil guys rushing over around me. The whole scuffle had taken mere seconds. My gaze dropped to my arm, taking in the thin streak of blood running toward my wrist from the scrape beneath my elbow… and then I noticed a few chunks of dried reddish mud on the floor under the car I'd scratched myself on.

"Wow," Slade said, sounding startled but also awed. Dexter was just staring at the scene. But Logan came marching past me like a tank bearing down on the guy sprawled by the far wall.

"Put your hands on her again, and you'll face something ten times worse," he snarled, his voice vibrating with more anger than I'd ever heard from him before. He'd pulled himself even taller, looming over my attacker with his extensive brawn on full display, what I could see of his expression taut with rage. "You'll wish you were never fucking *born*."

The man sputtered and then—in a spurt of bravery or stupidity, I couldn't tell—started to pull himself to his feet, glowering up at Logan. "You'd better get out of this shop or—"

Logan pushed closer so quickly I winced in anticipation for a strike, but he didn't lay a hand on the man. He just spoke as if through clenched teeth, menace dripping from his words. "Don't even think about it. Or maybe do. I'd just love an excuse to see how much I can make you suffer. She's lying on the floor bleeding, you prick. I think a little payback is in order."

Part of me wanted to point out that technically I was sitting up, and I wasn't actually bleeding very much, and also I'd already paid the jerk back with plenty of blows of my own. Part of me stayed frozen, struggling to process what I was seeing. I'd seen Logan pissed off, sure, but never so absolutely enraged. He sounded like he might be capable of almost anything.

It was scary… and it was also, against my will, a little thrilling. He was that furious on *my* behalf, because I'd been hurt. He sounded like he was prepared to pummel this guy to oblivion to defend me. How the hell was that even possible?

How the hell could I welcome the sight?

The logical side of my brain overrode the rest. I didn't want him getting into a fistfight over me with whatever other trouble that might bring. We were here to find my car, not to do battle—and I had reason to believe we were closer than we might have realized.

"Logan," I said, loud and clear to make sure he heard me. "My car's been here. The same mud—it's on the floor where they've got this one jacked up now."

Dexter knelt down beside me—checking my arm as if to confirm the scrape wasn't that bad before turning his attention to the floor, I noticed with a twinge of gratitude. He rubbed a bit of the dried mud between his fingers. "It's definitely the same stuff."

Logan's shoulders came down a smidge. He shot one last glare at my attacker and spun around to take in the rest of the space. Without another word, he was barging past the cars to a garage-style door at the back of the bay.

"Hey," the first mechanic protested, but his voice came out so weak even I wasn't concerned about him now.

"What are you going to do about it?" Slade asked him in a jaunty tone as he walked over to help me onto my feet. "Tell us we're *not* allowed to take our rightful property back?"

He let me stand on my own, and the rest of us hurried after Logan, who'd just hit the button to open the door. The steel surface whirred upward—and revealed a small parking lot in the back of the building with four vehicles parked in a row. The one at the farthest left had a familiar green hood.

My heart leapt. I dashed over to my Malibu and ran my hand over the side as if I needed to touch it to confirm it was really there. My hard-earned ride that I'd started to think I might never see again. It looked perfectly fine, not at all damaged, no more scratches or dents than had been there before it'd been stolen. A sigh of relief rushed out of me.

"For fuck's sake," Logan growled. He spun around as if to confront the mechanics, but all I wanted to do was get out of here, not linger in the awful parts of the confrontation.

I fished my keys out of my pocket. "I've got my fob. We don't need anything else from them. Can we just get going?" I paused. "Unless we should call the police and report it."

"It won't get us very far," Dexter remarked evenly. "Since you didn't report the car stolen already, the guys can easily claim *you* parked it here just now, or that you brought it in earlier to have work done. They're probably not the people who stole it anyway."

"No," Logan said, but there was an ominous note to his voice I didn't totally like. He shot a glower into the bay and then turned back to us, suddenly all business. "Dex, ride with Madelyn back to campus so she doesn't have to go alone. Slade and I will meet you there."

Dex nodded and moved to the passenger side as I clicked the button to unlock the door. I didn't really care about getting the police involved—I had my car back, and someone else could worry about catching the assholes who'd taken it if they kept up their shady practices.

But as shaky as I still was from the fight and the sudden discovery of my car, I couldn't help lingering over Logan's last words as I sank into the driver's seat. What did it matter to Logan whether I had to make the drive alone? Shouldn't he be jumping for joy that now I'd have no excuse to seek him out again?

Or was it possible that somewhere deep down, in the same place that rage had come from, I did still matter to him a little, no matter what he'd said to me yesterday?

And if I did, why was he working so hard at acting like I didn't?

CHAPTER
FOURTEEN

Madelyn

Dexter stayed quiet through the drive back, flipping through something on his phone, but I couldn't say I minded. My body was still buzzing with adrenaline after the confrontation in the mechanic shop, my mind whirling.

That guy had been so willing to use physical force to threaten me. What the hell else did they do in that place other than deal in stolen cars?

And where had the menace I'd seen from Logan come from? He'd always stood up to bullies—the fact that he'd done as much for me back in junior high was one of the main reasons I'd first developed a crush on him—but back then he'd done it with easy-going confidence and disarming words. His substantial physical presence had helped, but I'd never seen him go out of his way to be outright intimidating.

But then, I'd already realized that a lot had changed with him.

When I parked outside my residence building, a strange sense of resignation settled over me. This was it. I'd retrieved my car, and the Vigil's job was complete. No more verbal sparring with Logan, and no more heart-pounding adventures into the criminal underside of the city.

I knew it was for the best, but something tugged at my chest as I thought about going back to my comparatively mundane life with no idea what else these guys were getting into.

As Dexter pushed open the door to get out, nodding to the other guys who'd just pulled up in Logan's car across from us, I leaned over to open the glove compartment. Now that I knew how easily my car could be stolen, I'd like to put Dad's box somewhere that seemed a little less precarious. Stashed away in my dorm room seemed like a reasonable temporary solution.

The compartment swung open... and I simply stared.

There was the user's manual. There was my lip gloss and the first aid kit and mini flashlight I kept in the car for emergencies. A couple of folded papers were sitting on top of the manual, and I snatched them up.

My insurance documentation. The records that I'd been keeping inside Dad's box... which wasn't in the glove compartment at all.

I gaped at the opening for a few moments longer, as

if the black lacquer box might materialize before my eyes. Then I pawed at the other items in case it'd somehow gotten obscured behind them.

There was no denying it. The box wasn't there.

I swiveled in my seat, checking under both of the front seats and then peering into the back of the car. No sign of it. I popped the trunk and hurried around to check that too. It still held my spare tire and emergency blanket, but that was it. My stomach twisted.

Slade had sauntered over with a jaunty smile. "Those were some moves you used on that prick back at the shop. Where'd you learn how to do that?"

"Martial arts classes," I said automatically, my attention still focused on finding my treasured possession. "I took them for years. Wanted to learn how to defend myself."

Partly because I'd been ashamed when I'd realized how easily Logan had stood up for me back when we were kids. I hadn't wanted to be the weak, shrinking girl I'd become after Dad's death. Discovering my physical power had been one of the steps I'd taken toward becoming as strong as the boy who'd defended me—as strong as Dad would have wanted me to be. Not that I could admit that to my stepbrother now without him laughing in my face.

"You obviously learned well." Slade chuckled, but his expression turned more serious as I shoved down the lid of the trunk and he saw my face. "What's wrong?"

"My dad's box." I spun around to look at him and

the other two guys who'd joined him. "It's not in there. It's not anywhere."

The guys exchanged a glance. Logan frowned. "Are you—"

I jabbed a finger at him. "Don't you dare ask if I'm *sure*, Logan. I checked the glove compartment where I normally keep it, and all through the inside of the car, and the trunk. There's no reason for anyone to have taken it out of the glove compartment to begin with, but it isn't anywhere!"

He held up his hands. "All right, all right."

"Maybe the thieves chucked it out with a bunch of other stuff when they were preparing to pass the car on to the chop shop?" Slade suggested, rubbing his mouth.

I shook my head. "Nothing else is missing. I had a bunch of other things in the glove compartment and the trunk, and everything else is still there. They even took my insurance papers out of the box and left *those* behind." I swept my hair back from my face, my thoughts whirling. "Why would anyone take that? It didn't have anything else in it. It couldn't have been worth much money. It was only important to me because it was my dad's."

I'd rather the culprits had managed to scrap the entire car for parts but left that behind than taken the trinket box. It'd held so many memories… It'd been the one thing of Dad's I'd brought with me to college. This didn't make any sense.

Dexter knit his brow. He stepped past me to check the car over himself, brisky and efficiently—and without any of Logan's condescension, so I didn't mind that much. He straightened up with a shake of his head. "Definitely not in there. And given the other factors, it seems like whoever took it must have wanted the box specifically for some reason."

"But *why?*" I asked. "What the heck is going on here?" Had the thief already known they wanted the box before they'd stolen the car? Had I been targeted somehow? It sounded absurd, but I couldn't see why someone who didn't know me would think the box had any significance. It didn't look expensive.

But even as I sorted through those possibilities, I caught the shift of Logan's weight as he glanced at Slade and the tightening of Slade's mouth in return.

"I don't know," Logan said. "It's pretty strange."

Was it? Something about the look they'd exchanged had suggested they weren't totally surprised. I studied them. "Did something like this happen with the other cars?"

"We don't know what happened with the other cars, since we didn't work those cases." Logan's tone had turned firm. "Probably some idiot assumed the box was worth more than it looked like or that you had something valuable inside."

That didn't explain why they'd kept it after opening it and seeing what it did contain, or why they'd left all the other items behind if they'd been looking to sell off whatever they could, but maybe he was right.

I hugged myself, my nerves jittering. The loss of the car had felt bad enough, but the thought of someone going through the things inside, taking the one object that'd meant so much to me, was even more of an invasion.

"Did you talk to anyone else about that box?" Dexter asked with an analytical glint in his eyes.

"I mean, I might have mentioned it to my roommate, but it's not like it's the kind of thing that'd come up in regular conversation." My gaze slid between the three guys. "Even if I had, why would that make a difference? If someone heard me mention it, they should know it was only important for sentimental reasons."

Dexter gave an awkward shrug. Slade popped another cinnamon candy and clicked it thoughtfully against his teeth. The vibe had definitely changed between the guys. A sense of foreboding I couldn't totally explain rolled over me.

Logan squared his shoulders. "You don't have to worry about it. We'll find it for you just like we found the car. It'll probably be enough just to go back to the shop and convince the idiots there to cough it up."

Something about the way he said "convince" combined with his earlier aggressiveness sent an uneasy tingle down my back. "I'll come with you," I said. "I'm the only one who knows exactly what it looks like."

"Your sketch and description got the idea across just fine," he said, his voice hard as steel. "I don't want you setting so much as a toe in that place again after what that asshole tried to pull."

"I'm fine," I protested.

He grabbed my wrist and held up my arm, putting the scrape below my elbow on full display. "That's not fine. And he could have done worse."

The raw skin there still stung, but the little bit of bleeding had already stopped. I motioned to the front of my car. "I'll clean it up with my first aid kit and be good as new. It's just a scratch. I did worse to the asshole who attacked me."

"Yes, indeed, you did," Slade said with amusement, his gleeful grin only faltering when Logan glared at him, dropping my wrist. I regretted the loss of his warm hand more than I liked.

My stepbrother turned his attention back to me. "You have no idea what you're getting into, Madelyn. Scuffles like that are only the start. I'm not putting you in danger like that again. And if you're with us when we go out to handle shit like this, people are going to keep targeting you because you don't look like a threat. Next time you might not be able to fight your way out so easily."

"But you'll still be in danger then." I set my hands on my hips. "You're getting into it on my behalf. The least I can do is be there to help."

"It's not the same. We've gone through this kind of stuff dozens of times. We know how to handle criminals. You don't, no matter how much big talk you spew out. One wrong step, and you could get *really* injured. What would actually help the most is if you went back to your studies and pretended nothing's wrong until we deliver your Dad's box to you. And then nothing will be wrong."

I didn't know how to argue with the unshakeable certainty in his voice. It painted a picture that made me shiver.

I *had* been attacked, and I hadn't been prepared for the assault at all. My self-defense training had kicked in, thank God, but I definitely wasn't used to getting into fights like that. Would the guys' search really put them —and me—in that much more danger?

Remembering the situation in the mechanic shop, it wasn't difficult to believe. The way Logan had reacted to the attack had shown *he* was ready for possible violence. He hadn't hesitated to step in and show the jerk just who he was messing with. And Slade and Dexter had rushed in too.

What had they been through during past investigations that'd made them so confident dealing with that kind of aggression?

For a moment, the thought of doing what Logan asked—walking up to my dorm room, opening up one of my textbooks, and acting like none of this was going on—brought a wave of relief. I didn't *want* to be grabbed by strange men growling threats; I didn't want to be used as some kind of hostage.

But before that fear could fully take hold, my stubbornness kicked in.

I'd come this far. We were only looking for a simple decorative box, not illicit drugs or a weapon or something. The people who'd have taken it couldn't be *that* dangerous, could they?

And if they could be, then I wanted to know. I wanted to be standing right there with the guys like I had at the shop, where I *had* held my own, thank you very much.

I couldn't let Logan push me away again—not this time. It wasn't about him and whatever his reasons were for holding me at a distance. This was about me and something that mattered to me more than almost anything.

I raised my chin, fixing him with my steadiest gaze. "I don't care how dangerous this gets. I'm not helpless. I took care of myself today, and I can do it again."

Logan grimaced. "If your dad were here—"

Oh no, he didn't. I cut him off before he could take that idea any farther. "My dad *isn't* here. He's dead, and this box is one of the most important things I have left of him. And you never even knew him, so you have no reason to assume that he wouldn't agree with my decisions. He believed in me."

A flash of surprise crossed Logan's face, and I realized that my voice had risen as I spoke the words.

"Damn," Slade said with a low whistle, but I ignored him as I stared down Logan with narrowed eyes.

"We made a deal, and I'm not backing out of it, so the deal still stands. I'm staying on this investigation."

CHAPTER
FIFTEEN

Dexter

"So, no luck with the mechanics?" Madelyn said, sinking into one of the chairs at the central table in the Vigil office.

I thought she still looked a bit annoyed that we'd finally talked her out of going back to the shop with us to ask about her memento of her dad, even though Slade and I had promised emphatically that we'd keep her in the loop and have her along on less dicey parts of the investigation. When Slade had pointed out that the guy she'd pummeled might have a grudge against her now and be less likely to talk if she was around, she'd finally backed down.

It was much better that she hadn't been with us, though. There'd been threats Logan wouldn't have wanted to make, force he wouldn't have wanted to resort to when she was watching. That part of his reaction to her I at least partly understood. I wasn't totally comfortable with the means we resorted to in order to achieve our ends either.

But who was I to complain?

"They had no idea there'd ever been a box of any kind in the car," I told her, meeting her eyes for just a second. They were kind eyes, and pretty with that deep shade of blue—at least I thought so—but holding someone's gaze for more than a moment always sent a creeping sensation over my skin. It was easier to pretend I was occupied considering other things. "Whoever stole your Malibu must have taken the trinket box out before they dropped the car off at the shop. They left it with a note saying they'd be by to pick up the cash from selling the parts in a week."

Madelyn frowned, her smooth forehead furrowing. "Is that how chop shops normally operate?"

I shook my head. "Not from what I've seen. It's definitely unusual that they wouldn't come to a direct agreement about the price and all that. The thief was being particularly secretive."

"Are you sure we can trust anything those assholes said?"

"I saw no reason to doubt them," I said evenly. After the way Logan had intimidated them while he'd asked his questions, seeing the expressions on their faces, I was sure they'd been telling us the truth. He'd made them nervous, and nervous people made mistakes, but none of their body language or comments had given any hint that they were hiding something.

"Crap." Madelyn sighed and slumped in the chair, her fine blond hair sliding across her shoulders. "What now?"

"That's why I called you in." I flicked to the notetaking app on my phone. "Anything you can tell us about this box and its significance might help us narrow down the culprits. I know it belonged to your dad and approximately what it looks like. What did your dad use it for? Did he ever say anything noteworthy about it? Why did it seem special enough to him that you wanted to hold on to it?"

Madelyn rubbed her mouth, her eyes going out of focus as she reached into her memories. I could focus on her more easily now when she wasn't looking right back at me.

"I mean, like I said before, its value was all sentimental, as far as I know. It was always a fixture on his desk—even when he reorganized or got new furniture, it kept its spot right at the corner. I liked to pick it up and run my fingers over the design when I'd go in there to visit with him while he was working."

"Did he work from home a lot?" I asked.

She nodded. "Enough that he kept that small home office. For the more intensive research, he needed to be in the hospital or the lab he had ties to, of course, but when he was reading up on a subject or compiling notes or that sort of thing, he'd often do that at home. He said he wanted to be around as much as possible to see me growing up. That's why he didn't mind me dropping in. He'd say he was always happy to have an excuse to take a quick break."

She paused with an audible swallow. I felt abruptly awkward, not knowing what to say. I knew more about this situation than she had any clue about, and yet at the same time I had no idea what the details had looked like from her perspective.

"He died when you were pretty little, didn't he?" I said in what I hoped was a gentle tone.

Madelyn sucked in a breath and gave me a wry smile. "Yeah. I was eight. Maybe it's silly that it still affects me, but it was so sudden, and— It's hard not to think about what it'd be like if he were still here. He was a really great dad, always encouraging me and there when I needed him. It was an unexpected illness, came on suddenly and hit him really hard. We barely realized we were saying actual goodbyes before he was gone. It took me a long time to get back to feeling close to normal again."

"I'd imagine that's understandable."

"It doesn't help you find the box, though." She straightened her posture with an air of determination I was starting to see came naturally to her. "I'm not totally sure why he liked the thing so much. Maybe I'd have asked him once I'd gotten older and really thought about details like that. He'd have told me—he wasn't the kind of parent who'd brush off questions or give half-hearted answers to a kid. He always gave me his full attention."

"He does sound like a great dad." I wished my own parents had been more like that.

"Yeah. I just remember he told me it was his 'box of secrets.' A place where you could hide away important things. I told him I wanted something like that, and he swore we'd pick one out, but before we got around to doing that..."

She trailed off, but my mind had latched on to her earlier words with a surge of adrenaline. A "box of secrets" for hiding important things? That *was* the sort of thing someone might want to steal, wasn't it?

"Was it some kind of puzzle box then?" I asked, restraining my eagerness. My fingers were already itching to get my hands on it and figure out the tricks.

"I... I don't think so," Madelyn said. "Like with secret compartments and stuff? It opened like a normal wooden box, and I never found any other drawers or whatever. But I could have missed something, I guess. I didn't look that hard."

This was a puzzle about a puzzle, then. Playing right to my skills... But first we had to solve the part of the puzzle that would let me get my hands on the thing. If her dad had hidden something away in the box that no one had ever found—if someone out there had reason to believe he'd done that and that whatever he'd hidden was important...

I was so wrapped up in those speculations that Madelyn must have thought I'd totally zoned out. I barely remembered she was in front of me until she moved her hand toward my arm as if to tap it to get my attention.

The motion made me tense up before her fingers had even brushed my sleeve. Madelyn jerked her hand back with an apologetic grimace. She tucked it under the table on her lap. "I'm sorry. I know you don't really like the whole physical contact thing."

An embarrassed heat crept across my face. She must have noticed my awkwardness around touch back in high school. I didn't exactly like the idea of it having been that obvious, even though it was true. Sudden contact made my nerves jump, even if it was friendly.

I did my best to smile and make light of the situation. "I guess you must have wondered what was up with my friends getting permission before giving me even a high five and stuff like that."

Madelyn shrugged, seeming totally unfazed. "Everyone's entitled to their preferences. If Logan and Slade couldn't respect yours, they'd be crappy friends. I'll have to get into that habit of being more conscious about that stuff too."

She made it sound as if I wasn't weird at all. Which I knew wasn't true, because I'd gotten enough strange looks from other people at my reactions to a casual tap or nudge. My mom had often grumbled about how I'd stiffen up if she'd come in for a spontaneous hug.

Madelyn's acceptance was such a relief that a tickle of curiosity passed through my mind. Would I really mind it that much if she touched me? She definitely wasn't like any other woman I'd been around. Why didn't she judge me when so many other people did? She hardly knew me, and yet *she* treated me with more respect than people who'd been in my life for ages. And she wasn't just easy-going and kind—she was smart too. A whole puzzle all in herself.

Why was Logan so set on keeping her in the dark? Imagine what she might be able to figure out alongside us if she had the full picture.

I took a deep breath and shut down those thoughts. My first loyalty was to Logan, not to the woman in front of me. He'd made himself clear when he claimed that Madelyn would be in more danger if we involved her, and I wouldn't go behind his back and do that.

"Is there anything else I can do to help right now?" she asked.

"Not at the moment," I said with forced nonchalance. "I'll let you know when we're ready to take our next real steps."

Yes, Madelyn was a puzzle, and this entire situation seemed to be full of the kinds of puzzles that I'd usually devour and solve in a matter of hours. But I couldn't let myself be distracted from what was really important. I'd have to shut down my puzzle-addicted brain before it carried me off the deep end again. I might think Madelyn had the right to participate as much as Logan would let her, but I wasn't going to pull her into a scenario where she'd get hurt.

I wouldn't make that mistake again. I'd already dragged more people down with me than I'd ever wanted to.

CHAPTER
SIXTEEN

Madelyn

The line at the post office had me tapping my toes impatiently. An old man with a long beard had brought in a stack of letters that looked about a foot high and was now making the lone clerk weigh each of them to make sure he had the right postage before affixing the stamps to the upper right corner with painstaking care.

I'd been here for ten minutes, and I hadn't gotten any closer to mailing my package. My talk with Dexter this morning had left me feeling nostalgic for home and thinking fond thoughts of the parent I hadn't lost. I'd decided to stop by the chocolate shop in town I'd discovered Mom loved so I could pick up some truffles to send her.

My phone chimed with an incoming text—a

welcome distraction. I tucked the package with the chocolates under my arm and pulled out my phone.

What's up? Summer had written.

Not a whole lot, I typed back. *Have you ever been three people back in line behind a senior citizen who's sending letters to all their known relatives? I swear I could have gotten this package to my mom in less time if I'd driven home.*

The bubbles appeared at the bottom of the screen immediately, showing she was preparing her response. *I'll trade you. Have you ever been called a worthless waste of space for forgetting an order of fries for a table? Lunch shift is the worst.*

I winced inwardly. *There's a reason I never became a server at the diner with you.*

And there's a reason I never go to the post office. Order online and have stuff sent direct! That's the way to go.

My lips curled into a bemused smile. *Not everything can be ordered online, you know. Aren't you all about shop local?*

Only when I'm also keeping it local, she shot back with a winking emoji. Then she added, *It must be nice having your car back. No problems from the theft?*

I hadn't told her about the missing trinket box because I didn't want to worry her more. Maybe once it was found, I'd share my ongoing worries, but I didn't want to hear her tell me that I should just let it go.

I didn't *want* to let it go, and I didn't want to explain that to someone else. I'd pushed so hard the past few days with the guys, I couldn't bring myself to face convincing someone else.

Nope, I wrote. *Everything's working fine. Apparently the way they steal cars these days, with the modern models, they don't even hotwire them. So nothing got damaged.*

The old man finally handed over his stack of envelopes, and the line started moving again. The next woman briskly bought a pack of padded envelopes. *G2G*, I added to Summer, and tucked my phone away.

At the tap of footsteps behind me, I glanced over my shoulder instinctively. My heart skipped a beat just as the guy I found myself looking at raised his eyebrows at me.

"If it isn't Madelyn from the coffee shop," Beckett said with an amused glint in his gray eyes. I'd forgotten just how good-looking he was with his bright gaze and sharply regal nose beneath the artfully messy waves of his sandy-blond hair. Especially when he was giving me that subtly warm smile.

"If it isn't Beckett from the sidewalk outside the coffee shop," I replied in an attempt at being funny that sounded all wrong the second it'd come out, remembering exactly how we'd met on that sidewalk. "Did you get the stain out of your shirt?"

He held up his hand as if swearing in on a witness stand. "I promise you did no permanent damage, other than to my general focus."

"What's that supposed to mean?" I asked, already flushing a little at the teasing note in his voice.

His smile widened slightly. "I've been wondering

whether I'd cross paths with you again. Didn't expect to bump into you here, though."

"Yeah, I'm just—mailing something to my mom," I said, holding up the package and abruptly wondering if that sounded weird or childish. Weren't parents supposed to be the ones sending their kids stuff at college, not the other way around? Although Mom did send me plenty. But Beckett didn't know that.

He didn't show any outward reaction, just held up an oversized envelope of his own. "Business documents to mail. It's hard to believe some people still don't use email for that kind of thing."

"I guess there's something to be said for hard copies."

The space in front of me opened up, and the clerk motioned me over. A moment later, a second clerk joined her at the second register, and it ended up that I'd finished posting my package just as Beckett had paid for his registered mail. He walked over to the door with me, easing just a little ahead so he could open it for me.

"I *am* capable of opening doors on my own, you know," I said in a lightly ribbing tone. "Or even for you."

Beckett chuckled. "Read nothing into the gesture other than that I enjoy the chance to make your life a tiny bit easier. If you want to return the favor sometime, you're more than welcome to. Where are you off to now, Madelyn?"

Something about his presence set me at ease—his upbeat calm, the steady confidence with which he'd let the implied criticism roll off him. A lot of guys would have gotten their backs up if teased like that. And his attitude couldn't have been more different from Logan's grouchy cockiness.

"You can call me Maddie," I found myself saying. "I like that better—less stuffy-sounding. And I was just going to pop into the dollar store to grab a new pack of pens. Nothing exciting."

"I'm heading that way myself," Beckett said. "Do you mind if I join you?"

I'd actually been kind of hoping he'd offer, as much as I hated to admit that. I couldn't tell whether the store was really on his way or he was just saying that so we could talk more, but it was probably better not to read too much into that comment either.

As we set off along the sidewalk, I glanced at him sideways, thinking about what he'd said in the post office. "So, what kind of work do you do? I guess you must have graduated pretty recently. I mean, assuming you don't look way younger than you actually are." I bit my lip. Why did I keep putting my foot in my mouth with this guy? "Sorry, that probably sounded awful."

Beckett laughed. "No, it's a perfectly normal question. I don't know how old—or young—I look to you, but it sounds like you judged about right. I'm twenty-three. But I've been helping out with the family business since I was in my early teens, and I basically grew up in the middle of it, so it kind of feels like I've always had this job even if I only took it on full-time recently."

Maybe that explained part of his confidence—the fact that he'd always known what he'd be doing when he grew up, unlike so many of my college peers who seemed to be kind of drifting along, still undecided about everything… often down to their majors. That kind of certainty was a privilege a lot of people didn't have, but who was I to judge when I'd spent my whole life preparing to follow in my dad's footsteps with the interests he'd encouraged in me?

I felt comfortable enough to tap Beckett playfully with my elbow. "And am I allowed to ask what the family business is?"

"Oh, we've got our fingers in all sorts of pies. My dad and my grandpa before him were always looking for ways to expand and diversify. One of our main focuses is real estate development, which is an area I enjoy quite a bit. We've also got some holdings in manufacturing and transportation."

I blinked. "Wow. Sounds like it's a pretty big business." Not some mom-and-pop-type deal. But then, looking at him in his perfectly fitted suit and shiny shoes that I had to imagine cost way more than I'd ever spent on an item of clothing, that probably shouldn't have surprised me. It was just weird to think of a guy only three years older than me being established enough to be arranging major deals or whatever.

Beckett shrugged, but his smile shifted, turning a bit softer around the edges in a way that told me the enthusiasm in his voice was genuine. "It can get a little unwieldy at times, but I generally enjoy the challenge.

And seeing a development project move from an empty lot or a shell of a building into something people are actually going to use is pretty amazing."

"It's great that you enjoy it so much," I said.

Something flickered through his expression, but his voice stayed as steady and warm as before. "It's not all sunshine and roses. Some of the people I work with can be difficult, and a lot of them aren't too keen on taking orders from a 'kid.' But I know I'm proving myself."

"I admire that attitude," I told him honestly.

"You must have the same kind of determination when it comes to your career path," Beckett said, nudging me back. "Medical research isn't exactly a slacker job."

I laughed. "No, it's definitely not. But I guess it is a lot like you said. Knowing that I could work on something that's really going to make a difference to people, feeling like I'm building toward cures or treatments that could make their lives so much better or even save those lives... That makes it worth it."

"Exactly. I think I must have sensed that we had that sort of attitude in common when we first met, and that's why I wasn't willing to let you get away with just paying me off for a dry-cleaning bill. I don't run into a whole lot of people who really care about what they do and not simply getting a paycheck out of it."

I made a face. "Strangely that's not the selling point you make it sound like. Madelyn Silver: she works really hard."

Beckett grinned down at me with a fond expression

that made my pulse stutter giddily. "Oh, I think there's a lot more to appreciate about you than just that, Maddie. And if I'm lucky, maybe you'll give me the chance to uncover more of it."

Okay, he was definitely flirting, right? I hadn't been totally sure with some of his earlier comments, because random guys didn't normally come up to me out of the blue and hit on me. Mom always said it was because I tended to look too serious for them to think it'd work, but she *was* my mom, so she had to make it sound like it wasn't anything actually off-putting about me.

I couldn't think of any other good reason for Beckett to not just have helped me with my groceries the other day but also be joining me on the grand adventure of popping into the dollar store, though. And that grin… It reminded me a little of Slade's, except his always felt partly joking, more playful than committed to a pursuit. Beckett made it sound like he wanted more than to just goof off a bit.

The thought of Slade drew me up short even as heat tickled across my face. Did I *want* Beckett to flirt with me—and to flirt back? My feelings for Logan were still a muddle, and I'd almost made out with Slade at the club the other night.

But was that so wrong? *Live a little, girl*—that was what Summer would have told me. Nothing was happening with Logan, and I sure as hell shouldn't put any interest I felt for another guy on the back burner because of him. And I had no idea where things were going with Slade, if anywhere.

I could play the field. It was *nice* to feel like a guy as together as Beckett saw something to admire in me. I definitely found him pretty impressive so far, inside and out.

I grinned back at him, hoping my jittering nerves didn't show in my expression. I might *want* to flirt, but that didn't mean I was any kind of expert at it.

"I think that could be arranged," I said.

"Getting my hopes up, huh? Thankfully you don't look like a heartbreaker."

I couldn't hold back a snort—or the comment that tumbled out of me. "Usually it's the other way around."

Oh, shit, why had I blurted that out? Now I sounded pathetic. I snickered as if I could pretend I'd been kidding, but Beckett's grin had faded.

"Has someone been jerking you around?" he asked, cool and even but with a firmness that suggested he thought he could do something about it if I said yes. His sudden protectiveness sent a heady shiver down my spine. "Was it one of those guys you mentioned hanging out with?"

"No, no," I said quickly, even though I'd mostly meant Logan. Damn it, why did he have to screw up even this? "It was a bad joke."

Beckett studied me for a second but then smiled again, to my relief. "Good. Because I might not know you that well yet, but I can already tell you deserve better than a broken heart."

I swallowed thickly. Funny how he could say that so

easily, and Logan who'd known me so much longer hadn't batted an eye at breaking it.

The bright yellow sign of the dollar store beamed at us from the corner. I slowed as we reached the entrance, feeling abruptly shy. "Well, this is me."

Beckett turned toward me, so close with his handsome face intent on mine that a waft of heat rushed through my body. His voice dipped lower. "Then it's time for me to try my luck. Have dinner with me tomorrow evening?"

"Um." Yes, I was a straight-A student, but somehow I'd lost all my words faced with that question. "You mean like a date?"

I could have smacked myself in the forehead, but I had to clarify, just to be sure. Beckett's renewed smile showed no sign of offense.

"I'm just looking to see how much else we have in common and find out all the other fascinating things about you. And if that sparks into something more, I'm not going to argue. I'm happy to call it a date if that doesn't make you feel pressured to do anything more than enjoy some good food and conversation."

I had a hard time imagining this guy putting on the pressure like a randy high school dude. I hesitated for just a second longer with a brief thought of Logan and the Vigil guys—but I didn't owe any of them anything, especially not my jerk of a stepbrother. Why shouldn't I have some fun and see where this could go?

I beamed back at Beckett with a leap of my heart. "It's a date, then."

CHAPTER
SEVENTEEN

Logan

I parked across the street from the mechanic shop just before closing and paused to make sure I couldn't see any customers through the grimy front window. Then I strode across the street and pushed past the door, letting all the menace I could summon rise to the surface.

It wasn't hard. These pricks had lied to us about having Madelyn's car and then tried to hold her hostage—the one asshole had left her *bleeding*. My jaw clenched just remembering the smear of blood on her arm.

Last time I'd come here, I'd only talked to them, asking them about the trinket box. But we hadn't turned up any other leads, and I was almost glad to have the excuse to beat some more answers out of them. I wasn't giving them the chance to consider lying through their teeth this time.

We were getting to the bottom of this before Maddie faced anything worse than what these miserable lowlifes had already done to her.

One of the mechanics from before was just shutting down the computer at the reception desk. He glanced up at me with a startled expression before his eyes narrowed. "You—"

I didn't give him the chance to complain about my arrival. I lunged around the desk, caught him by the front of his shirt, and heaved him toward the door to the mechanic bay.

He was at least ten years older than me, but I was bigger and stronger. My shove propelled him right into the door, which popped open on impact. As he staggered, I stormed after him. With another abrupt push, he was stumbling onto his ass in the bay.

There was only one other mechanic still on duty this late in the evening—the big guy who'd grabbed Madelyn. "Hey!" he shouted, rounding one of the two cars currently set up there, and hesitated for just a second when he saw who the intruder was.

I smiled at him with bared teeth, the image of his thick arms swinging around Madelyn flashing behind my eyes and provoking a fresh surge of rage. Oh, I was really looking forward to this now. I hadn't really paid him back yet.

The first guy scrambled to his feet and took a swing at me. I smacked his fist to the side and clocked him in the chin. As he swayed and swore, grabbing his face, the second guy charged at me.

He was a little more of a challenge, with nearly as much muscle on him as I had. But he didn't have a raging fury driving his attack. He managed to land a punch to the side of my chest, but then I was kneeing him in the gut and tossing him into the side of the nearest car.

He glanced off it and hurtled back toward me. The first guy darted at me at the same time.

I dodged out of the way and slammed my knuckles into the smaller guy's throat. As he sputtered, I stomped my heel into his shin hard enough that the crack of breaking bone echoed off the bay's high ceilings.

You couldn't go easy on guys like these—the kind of guys who thought it was okay to beat up on an innocent woman. They needed to know just how much I meant business and just how little they'd get away with if they tried to pull anything over on me.

The guy fell with a strangled whimper. He wouldn't be getting up anytime soon. He fumbled in his pocket for a phone, but I kicked it out of his hand, snapping at least one finger in the process. The phone rattled across the floor to the other side of the room.

Now I had only one prick to deal with. A prick who was bearing down on me at this exact instant.

"Who the fuck do you think you are, kid?" the big guy snarled.

"Someone you're going to regret ever having messed

with," I shot back, deflecting his swings with only a faint pain radiating through my blocking forearm.

He whipped his fist around fast enough to smack me in the side of the head. I reeled for a second, but I'd been hit worse. I bobbed and wove like I'd learned in my kickboxing sparring sessions and caught him with my knee a second time, ramming it into his side.

From the pained grunt that burst from the guy's mouth, I'd cracked at least one of his ribs, as I'd intended. He clutched at his chest but hurled his other fist toward me. But he was off-balance now.

I swept my leg into his calf and knocked him off his feet. As he sprawled on the floor, I kicked him in the back of the head for good measure, hard enough to leave him groaning.

Touch my girl again, and you won't have any breath left to groan with, you fucking jackass, I thought, biting back the words. A lingering ache spread through my skull from where he'd hit me, but it was already fading. I'd dealt it back ten times over.

"What the fuck do you want, man?" the smaller guy rasped from where he was still crouched on the cement floor, bent awkwardly over his broken leg. "You got your car back. We told you we didn't take anything out of it."

"Maybe I don't believe you." I aimed a light kick at his leg, just enough to send another spear of agony through the limb. "You really can't remember a single thing about who brought it in? Even when I jog that memory of yours?" I turned to the bigger guy, who was starting to sit up, and brought my heel down on the ribs I'd kicked earlier. "I can keep jogging it as long as I need to," I added as he slumped onto his back again with a hiss of pain.

"There's nothing to remember," the first guy mumbled in a panicked voice that sounded genuine enough. He was afraid I wouldn't believe him, not constructing a story. I'd been through this kind of interrogation often enough to tell the difference. "It was just dropped off; none of us saw who left it. Fucking weird, but you can't blame us for that."

I snatched up a wrench off a nearby shelf of tools and flipped the heavy metal tool in my hand, glowering down at the guy who'd grabbed Maddie. Oh please, do give me an excuse to bash your nose in and fracture every bone in your body with this thing.

"What about you?" I demanded. "Did you notice anything?"

The guy's bravado had finally vanished, a flicker of fear passing through his eyes. He still grimaced as he spat out, "I don't know anything. You're fucking crazy, kid."

I smirked again, leaning into his claim, knowing it would unnerve him. "It doesn't seem very smart to give a crazy person a hard time, does it?" Then I whacked him in the shoulder with the wrench, not hard enough to do more than lightly bruise, just to show him I wasn't afraid to use it.

The man growled a curse word and screwed up his face. "He already told you. The car was just dropped off.

No one's come around about it. I fucking wish they'd taken it someplace else."

Fair enough. I tapped the wrench against my open palm, my gaze darting between the two mechanics. "What about your regular clients, the ones you *do* know? Is there anyone who you work with regularly who's brought in other stolen cars like hers?"

"Our clients don't know shit about your car," the bigger man grumbled.

"That's not what I asked," I reminded him, aiming another kick at his ribs.

"Fuck," he sputtered, his head lolling back for a moment as he fought through the pain. "We don't have any consistent regulars on that side of the business. Different people come by—maybe some of them work for the same organization. We don't ask questions. We don't get ID."

Well, that wasn't completely surprising, even if it wasn't all that useful. "What about new people?" I asked. "Has anyone you've never dealt with before come in asking questions or sniffing around?"

"You mean like you and your shitty friends?" the big guy snarked.

I slammed the wrench into his kneecap to remind him just how shitty I could be. "Like us, or just seeming more interested than usual in your business in any way. Answer the fucking question."

"No," he grated out. "I haven't noticed anyone like that, or I'd happily send you off to hassle them instead of us, you maniac. Have you checked out the junk yard?

That's the main chop shop in town. He knows a lot more people than us."

I brought down the wrench on the man's other kneecap. His shout of pain felt good as it drowned out the small cry of pain I'd heard from Maddie when she fell. Each of his sounds of discomfort warded away my memories of Maddie's a little at a time. "Right now I want to hear from you assholes, not anyone else."

"Man, we're telling you all we know," the smaller guy said raggedly.

I was becoming increasingly sure that was true, but I couldn't let this go. I needed some kind of direction, something that brought us closer to finding that box and keeping Madelyn away from thugs like these for good.

Maybe they were connected to the larger case in ways that hadn't even occurred to us before. I cast a narrow glance at both of the men. "What do you know about Southwestern Regional Memorial Hospital?"

I didn't even need a verbal response to that question as they looked amongst themselves, confusion written across both of their faces.

"Never heard of it," the big guy said. "What the hell does that have to do with anything?"

"I'm asking the questions here. Do you know anything about a man named Evan Silver?"

More visible confusion. "You're fucking insane, man," the smaller guy said. "What the hell are you going on about now?"

I couldn't help pushing one more time. "What about the Baldwin file?"

"Do we look like file clerks?" the big guy grumbled, and coughed out a grunt when I jabbed the toe of my shoe into his side. "Fucking hell. We have no idea what you're talking about."

"Sure you don't," I said. "But the car didn't drop down from heaven. *Someone* brought it around, someone picked this place. So I guess I'll just have to keep laying into you until one of you comes up with something useful."

I brought the wrench down on the shoulder I'd already hit, knowing it'd be tender, and gave the man a vicious grin. Then I turned to the smaller man, waving the tool threateningly. He outright cringed—and I saw a desperate spark light in his eyes.

"There was something a little weird!" he gasped out. "I almost forgot. I don't know if it had anything to do with that stupid car, but maybe…"

"Just spit it out," I ordered.

He winced at the threat in my tone. "I—I noticed a couple of guys scoping out the shop early one morning when I was out by the street finishing off a cigarette. It was a few weeks ago, way before the car turned up. I didn't think to connect the two. But I'd never seen them before, and I wondered why they were checking out the place."

I waggled the wrench again, a flare of hope filling my chest. This expedition might not have been for nothing after all. "Describe them."

"I didn't see them clearly… They were wearing hooded jackets and shades. Definitely guys, a couple of them. But their car—it was vintage. That was part of the reason I noticed them. They drove off in it less than a minute after I spotted them."

Now there was a lead we could use.

"What model?" I demanded, raising the wrench one more time in warning. "Tell me every detail you remember."

CHAPTER
EIGHTEEN

Madelyn

We walked two blocks from where the Vigil guys had parked Logan's car, through a middle-class residential neighborhood that was mostly quiet in the late morning. The empty driveways and vacant lawns suggested almost everyone who lived here had gone off to work or school.

The guys hadn't told me what exactly we were doing in this part of the city, only that they'd found a potential connection to my car thief. They slowed when we reached a two-story home with neat flowerbeds out front and white wicker furniture on the small porch. Then they walked along the narrow path between it and the neighboring house to the backyard as if they belonged there.

I hurried along with them, curiosity and

apprehension nibbling at me in unison. "You think the person who stole my car—or the box—lives here?" I whispered, knitting my brow as I took in the backyard with its well-maintained lawn and cedar patio furniture. Obviously you couldn't identify a thief from a glance, but I hadn't expected a criminal's house to look quite this tidy and ordinary. I could have imagined one of Mom's friends living here.

"We think this person is involved somehow," Logan said, low and terse. "Maybe not directly. But there was someone suspicious checking out the mechanic shop not long before your car was dropped off, and the car they were driving is registered to this address."

"How did you find *that* out?" I asked.

He shrugged, not meeting my eyes. "It's amazing what you can learn if you just ask around."

He obviously wasn't going to tell me more than that, but I wasn't too worried about that, only annoyed. I had trouble believing he was going to badger a stranger without a solid reason. Even so... "Will they tell us anything? They don't even know us."

Slade tapped his elbow against mine as we approached the back door. "The woman who lives here doesn't need to tell us anything. She's at work. We're just going to take a little look around." He grinned at me.

"*What?*" I clapped my hand over my mouth after the question burst out louder than I expected, my eyes darting toward the neighboring houses. The high wooden walls obscured all view of us except from one second-story window next door, and it was covered by thick curtains.

But what if someone noticed? The guys couldn't seriously be planning on—

Dexter was already kneeling by the back door, pulling a couple of slim metal tools from his pocket. I couldn't help gaping as he worked them into the lock.

"What if we get caught?" I hissed.

Logan shot me a look that felt like a dare. "It's just a little light breaking-and-entering. We're not going to hurt anyone or damage anything. We're only looking for information. You want your dad's trinket box back, don't you?"

He was probably hoping that I'd back down, turn tail and run so they could continue the investigation on their own. No doubt he wouldn't have brought me along at all if Dexter hadn't updated me as promised.

I clamped my mouth shut, my teeth on edge. My heart was thumping faster. I did want Dad's box—I wanted to know what was going on with the whole theft. I just hadn't realized we'd do something quite this illegal to get there. But the guys were acting like they'd carried out operations like this dozens of times.

What the hell *had* Logan been up to all these years since he'd pulled away from the family?

Whoever lived in this house was a criminal or had some association with one, I told myself as the lock clicked and Dexter stood with a satisfied smile. It wouldn't hurt them for us to look around. The guys seemed sure no one was home.

If I didn't trust them at least this much, what the hell was I doing here in the first place?

Dexter tugged the door open, and the guys marched inside. I followed at the back of the line, resisting the urge to hug myself. My stomach had knotted, but as we stepped into the narrow kitchen where the sweet scent of syrup hung in the air from whatever the owner had for breakfast, a little thrill shot through my chest too.

We were sneaking into someone else's life, getting a glimpse of a stranger that most people never did. Maybe we'd discover things no one else knew about her. Maybe I'd get some answers about why I'd been targeted.

We were taking control of the situation, and something about that felt right even though I knew the cops would have disagreed.

"What are we looking for?" I whispered.

"Anything suspicious," Slade said, already riffling through a stack of mail on the kitchen counter.

"The homeowner's name is Melinda Hughes," Dexter elaborated. "She's divorced and has lived alone since her kids moved out several years back, so she's the only one who's been residing in the house for a while. If you see any documents addressed to someone with a different name, we'll want to take a closer look at those. Or anything related to cars or pawn shops or that sort of thing."

Okay, I guessed that gave me a general idea. I crept deeper into the house, down a hall that led to a combined living-dining room. There were a couple of papers on the dining table, but on closer inspection I found they were only takeout menus. Maybe Melinda Hughes had ordered in dinner last night.

Dexter walked past me, snapping pictures of just about everything in sight. I got a little more into the search, easing up the sofa cushions to peek underneath, checking behind the chairs in the living room for anything that might have fallen, always careful to set things back as they'd been before. My shoes rasped softly over the thick carpet.

"If this woman isn't the thief herself, how could she be connected?" I asked.

Logan had moved to the front hall, flipping through a calendar that hung on the wall there. "So far I'm not seeing any sign of her being a criminal herself, so I'd guess that the actual perp is using her address as a cover. It's a pretty common tactic. He's probably a relative— son or nephew or cousin. Something like that."

He sounded a little less annoyed now that I'd gone along with the plan. Maybe getting down to work distracted him from how pissed off he was that I was working alongside him. I had to admit there was something satisfying about taking concrete action.

"We don't want to stay here any longer than necessary," Dexter reminded us.

Logan nodded. "Why don't you and I check the basement? Slade and Madelyn, head upstairs and split up to check the bedrooms and whatever else is up there. We'll cover more ground that way." He was all firm efficiency now, with an authoritative air that confirmed he was the unofficial leader of the group.

I slunk up the stairs, the back of my neck prickling with both anxiety and eagerness. What if I found the crucial clue? The longer we spent in the house, the less it felt like an intrusion and the more like some kind of detective game.

The first room at the top of the stairs was a bedroom. I scanned it as I heard Slade come up the stairs after me and head down the second-floor hallway. This room might have once belonged to one of the kids Dexter had mentioned, but it appeared to have been redone as a guestroom. The plain dresser and bedframe showed no signs of personality, and nothing hung on the walls with their leaf-print wallpaper.

I tugged open the drawers on the dresser and checked the closet, only confirming my suspicions. There was nothing stashed away here except for a couple of baggies of lavender potpourri. A shoe box under the bed got me briefly excited, but it only held… a pair of shoes.

The next room over must have been the master bedroom. It felt infinitely more lived in. The dark, rustic furniture set held a scattering of possessions, from a change bowl with a stick of lip balm and a couple of hair clips on the dresser to a few books stacked haphazardly on the bedside table.

I checked all of the drawers, shifting the contents as little as possible and tucking them back as I'd found them. None of the clothes or other belongings looked at all out of the ordinary for a woman who was my mom's age or older. As I finished my perusal of the last piece of furniture, an uncomfortable weight settled in my gut. I sat gingerly on the edge of the bed, grappling with it.

I'd thought we were justified in coming in here, that we'd find something that'd point to the criminal who'd invaded *my* life. But she seemed to be a totally normal woman. I couldn't shake the growing sense that we weren't accomplishing anything other than violating her privacy unnecessarily. We didn't belong in here any more than she'd belong in our homes.

Slade poked his head through the doorway. "Anything in here?"

I shook my head, my throat too tight for me to speak. Slade took in my expression and slipped into the room, a softer smile playing with his lips. "Aww, don't look depressed about it. Here, I can cheer you up."

He swung into a swift spin on his prosthetic leg, turning the movement into a brief jig of a dance and dipping into a deep bow at the end. I couldn't suppress a snort of laughter despite my dwindling spirits, but as he glanced up with a grin, my uneasiness wrapped around me again.

Slade sank down onto the bed next to me and grasped my hand. "Okay, looks like I'd better get serious. What's bothering you?"

I grimaced. "I just feel really weird having broken in here and poking around in all her stuff, and we haven't even found anything to connect her to my car or the box."

"Hey, first time jitters totally make sense." He squeezed my hand. "And sometimes leads don't take us anywhere. We have to follow them, though, because we never know which ones *will* pay off. It's a little trial and error. We haven't done any harm here, right?"

"We haven't," I had to agree. And his words made me feel better for another reason. "It's a lot like medical research that way. We have to test every possible hypothesis to make sure we get to the right—or the best—answer." Framing it that way in my head soothed my discomfort a little.

Slade chuckled. "Only a brainiac would compare breaking and entering to science." But he made the remark sound like a compliment rather than a criticism.

I couldn't resist teasing him right back. "I don't think you're in any position to be calling *me* a brainiac, Mr. 'I know a hundred languages.'"

Slade winked at me. "It's cool to know languages. It's nerdy to know science. I'm proud of not being a nerdy brainiac."

I elbowed him. "Just a cool one, huh? We'll see how cool you think I am when I come up with the cure for cancer or something."

"Oh, I already think you're very cool." He raised my hand and pressed his lips to my knuckles, his dark eyes sparkling at me. "You know, Logan and Dex are still searching around downstairs. I can think of other ways I could distract you from your guilty conscience."

A blush warmed my cheeks. "Like what?" I had to ask.

He simply smirked and tilted my hand so he could kiss my palm. His fingers tightened around mine as he brought his lips to the underside of my wrist, where the contact provoked a tingle that had me swallowing a gasp.

He charted a path up my arm, every kiss tender and deliberate, leaving plenty of opportunity for me to pull away if I wasn't into it. But with each brush of his mouth, more desire unfurled low in my belly, washing away my concerns just like he'd promised. Heat coursed up my arm and through the rest of my body.

How far was he going to take this?

But even as the giddiness of that question raced through me, something in me hesitated. My feelings about Logan were a mess. And I had a date with Beckett tonight. Should I be this into another guy touching me like this? How could my feelings be so fickle?

Slade reached my shoulder and pecked the peak. My pulse hiccupped as he scooted closer and dipped his head toward my neck, but every particle in my body was screaming to let him continue.

Why shouldn't I? I hadn't made any commitments to anyone, so I wasn't betraying anyone. And God, this felt good. Other than a couple of disastrous first dates in my first year of college, I hadn't kissed *anyone* in two years. I had some time to make up for, right?

My head tilted to the side of its own accord, offering Slade better access. He hummed approvingly and brought his lips to the side of my neck, nipping the skin lightly before pressing a more emphatic kiss there.

I bit my own lips against a whimper. Heat coiled between my legs into a deepening ache.

When Slade raised his head, I didn't hesitate again. I leaned in and met him halfway for our first real kiss.

Slade tucked his hand around the back of my neck, parting his lips just slightly as he drew me against him. My fingers clutched the front of his shirt, all the rest of me absorbed in his passionate claiming of my mouth. His tongue flicked out to tease across my bottom lip. The cinnamon flavor that laced it set me even more on fire.

His other hand dropped to my waist. At his tug, I found myself straddling him. Our bodies seared against each other, his arm sliding around my waist, our chests pressed together, and his mouth claiming mine. I had the embarrassing urge to grind right into him like I was starved for sexual contact. Although technically I was.

Slade trailed his hand down from my neck over my chest. He stroked the curve of my breast with the same caution he'd showed in his initial kisses, and then cupped it completely when I didn't recoil. His thumb swiveled over my nipple through the layers of fabric, and I let out a needy sound into his heated mouth.

He massaged my breast more eagerly, his mouth outright plundering mine, and the intensity of the moment was so overwhelming that I didn't fully register the creak of the stairs until a few seconds after the sound had first reached my ears.

I jerked back, sliding off Slade's lap. "Someone's coming up."

My gaze darted toward the door, half anticipating

one of the other guys glancing in, realizing what we'd been up to from the guilty flush burned into my cheeks.

Slade nuzzled the side of my head. "I know Logan can put on a scary front, but you don't need to be afraid of him getting angry. I survived his dance-floor interruption just fine."

The amusement in his tone brought my attention back to him. "Are you only doing this to irritate Logan?"

Slade laughed. "Riling him up is a benefit, sure. Can't let him get too cocky."

All the heat fled my body in the wake of a wash of cold. I might not have made commitments to anyone, including Slade—I might have figured this could just be fun in the moment—but the admission horrified me more than I'd expected. I'd assumed Slade was at least into it because he enjoyed making out with *me*, not because of how his friends would react.

I pushed myself farther away from him on the bed, my blush all embarrassment now, my stance tensing awkwardly. "We'd better stop then, because I actually like *you*."

Slade froze, looking oddly surprised, and then caught my hand. He studied my expression with unexpected intensity. "I didn't mean I don't like you, Maddie. I was just kidding around about the Logan thing. Hell, I think you're amazing."

"Oh." I had no idea how to feel, but the sincerity in his voice set off a warm glow inside me. I couldn't help smiling, even though I was still confused. "Well… good."

He arched his eyebrows, more of his usual playfulness coming back. "I promise anything that happens between us is going to be about you and me and how awesome you are, not anyone else. And if you're actually up for more than just an occasional fun distraction…"

Before I could decide how to respond to that, Dexter's voice carried up the stairs. "Hey, guys, you'd better take a look at this."

CHAPTER
NINETEEN

It was hard to pinpoint exactly what made Maddie so attractive. When I'd first seen her, I'd pegged her as a pretty but unexceptional college student. The V-neck sweater and fitted dress pants she'd worn for our date hugged her trim curves perfectly, but that wasn't all that made the difference either.

It was her smile, I decided, smiling back at her across the restaurant table. The way a dimple formed on just one cheek, the way her dark blue eyes sparkled when she laughed, the self-deprecating note that'd crept into her voice as she related a story from her high school days, which let me know she wasn't trying to brag, just sharing a little of herself.

She took a sip of her water and continued her story. "One of the worst was the head gym teacher, who also coached a bunch of the sports teams. Every time we walked into the gym, he'd scrutinize our outfits and then dress code any student he didn't agree with. But it was only the girls. We couldn't wear T-shirts that showed any of our shoulders or had a neckline lower than an inch below our collarbone, but he'd let the guys get away with basketball jerseys and stuff like that. None of us were trying to flaunt anything. It just got hot in there, especially late in the spring."

My smile widened, sensing retribution to come. Maddie had started this line of conversation by admitting she'd been quite a crusader for justice in her teen years. "So what did you do about it?"

Maddie ducked her head briefly in apparent embarrassment, though why she'd be embarrassed about sticking up for herself and her fellow students was beyond me. I guessed girls always had people come down on them harder for speaking up and demanding attention too.

Fucking ridiculous. It'd been a couple of women who'd taught me a lot of what I knew about being a force to be reckoned with in the world, and I'd have had a lot more than harsh words for anyone who'd tried to knock them down a peg.

"One day in June it was just sweltering," Maddie said, "and I got fed up. I wore a sleeveless shirt with a neckline that was just a smidge too low, and I brought a measuring tape with me to class. Sure enough, the teacher zeroed right in on me and demanded I go to the office. So I handed him the measuring tape in front of the whole class and said I wasn't going anywhere until he measured me and the two guys from the basketball team who'd come in their jerseys and proved that my shirt was somehow less acceptable than theirs."

A chuckle burst out of me. "I bet he wasn't happy about that."

Maddie's smile turned a little softer at the memory. She might feel awkward about it, but I could tell part of her was proud of the stands she'd taken.

"Nope. Especially because the guys' jerseys were at least an inch lower cut than mine, and the straps were a little thinner, so he had no ground to stand on. He tried to get all intimidating and insist that I go anyway, but my best friend was filming the whole thing on her camera… We both went and showed the principal how he'd acted, and he got a formal reprimand. And they adjusted the dress code so girls could wear thick-strapped tank tops for gym class." She cast me a cautious glance as if checking whether I was put off by the account. "We might have threatened to take the video to the local news if they didn't."

I clapped my hands lightly in a show of applause. This woman might not have come from the gritty sort of background my former mentors had, but she had plenty of guts, no doubt about it. "Sounds like you handled it perfectly."

Maddie blushed. "I mean, that's not how everyone saw it. I was a lot to handle back then. I'm sure I stressed my mom out with all the campaigns I took up against one thing or another, clashing with teachers and all that. And it's because I was so hard-headed about this stuff that I ended up pissing one teacher off enough to screw up my grades for college admissions."

I dug my fork into my pasta. "Everyone is difficult in high school. It's the age for it, isn't it? I wasn't an easy kid—that's for sure."

I'd intended that comment to prompt a question of her own, one that would let me tease the subject I was most interested in without asking anything too pointed. It worked. Maddie popped a bit of her glazed chicken into her mouth and raised her eyebrows at me. "And how were you difficult, Beckett? I sense some juicy stories."

It was almost too easy. A pang of guilt jabbed me in the stomach over the way I was manipulating her.

It was my job. I needed to know for sure whether the guys she was associating with were any kind of threat and whether she was mixed up in that threat with them. If I didn't pursue every possible avenue toward getting that information, then I'd be letting down every man and woman working under me.

But there was no denying that I saw Maddie as a hell of a lot more than a source of information. I'd already been intrigued by her before I'd asked her out, and the more we talked, the more admiration trickled through my chest.

I'd met a lot of people in my line of work, but no one who had quite the mix of daring and sweetness that she did. She was a fighter, but a genuinely moral person at the same time.

Which meant she might not give me the time of day

if she knew the full extent of my line of work, but I shoved that thought aside. That was a problem for another day, quite possibly for never. For all I knew, she might not want to entertain my advances beyond this date.

Giving her a playful smirk, I ate a mouthful of the pasta, letting the tangy rosé sauce coat my tongue as she waited. Anticipation worked wonders.

In reality, I'd spent all of a day in a public high school, and that visit had only been for the sake of learning about the son of someone my dad needed to target. I'd always been homeschooled by my dad's people and then in the thick of our kind of business, but I had enough of a gist to transpose a real story from my teens into a more appropriate setting.

"There was this bully at my high school who was terrorizing a lot of the kids," I said. "His dad worked with mine, and I knew my father wouldn't want me to intervene and potentially cause trouble at his job. But I hated seeing what he was doing to people, and I couldn't help thinking in the long run it'd be better to do something about it than not. I guess you know that feeling, like something needs to happen and you can't just stick your head in the sand?"

"Yeah," Maddie said softly, her gaze fixed on my face with an avidness that urged me on. I found I wanted to impress *her*, even if that wasn't the main reason I was telling this story.

"Well, I threw myself headfirst into the situation," I went on. "There was a group of students who'd started pushing back against the bully, but I knew some things they didn't about him that would help make him stand down. At first they didn't take me seriously, because I was a few years younger than them, but after I proved I could help, it was obvious we could accomplish a lot more working together."

I watched Maddie's expression carefully for any flicker of recognition at that kind of dynamic. Had she joined forces with that trio of guys to tackle something she saw as wrong in the city? Something to do with my and my father's business dealings, though she wouldn't have realized it was connected to me?

But her main response was to knit her brow. "How did your dad take it?"

Of course she'd worry about that. She wasn't just morally good but also compassionate.

I grappled with how to answer the question, because the basic answer was, *Not well at all.* But I didn't want to turn this into a venting session about my family issues.

"He didn't get any backlash at work," I said, sticking with a version that was brief but still somewhat accurate. "But he was frustrated that I'd gone behind his back. Things were a bit tense for a while, but I knew I'd done the right thing. And I made some lifelong friends who've still got my back if I need them."

We wouldn't get into how tense things still were at home.

If Maddie related my story to her own life, she didn't give any indication. "I'm sorry you had to go against him anyway," she said. "My mom was always supportive… I don't know what I'd have done if something I felt I needed to do conflicted with what she'd have wanted."

I shrugged. "All's well that ends well." I wished I could have left it there, but I had to give this line of inquiry every possible shot. "Are you taking up new crusades at the university?"

Maddie shook her head. "Not really. I mean, I'm sure if something really awful came up, I wouldn't be able to ignore it, but I'm not letting myself get distracted by the little things. Keeping up with my studies takes too much of my time and energy."

I cocked my head. "You don't seem like the type of woman who would let things go so easily."

Her eyes flickered around the room for a moment, and I longed to know exactly what she was thinking at that moment. "Don't get me wrong—I'm not going to stand by if something horrible goes down in front of me, but that hasn't happened so far. And I know that getting my degree means I'll be able to fix other kinds of injustices in the future, so I don't feel bad prioritizing it."

"Fair enough. There are various advocacy groups on campus, from what I've heard. I suppose you could join up with one of them if you wanted to get a little crusading out of your system."

"Good point." Maddie waved her fork at me. "Since I only transferred here a few months ago and I've been busy catching up and getting settled in, I haven't really looked into that stuff yet."

I didn't pick up on any deception in her answers. She was being perfectly straightforward with me. A sense of certainty filled my chest.

Whatever her friends—or acquaintances, or whatever they were to her—were up to, whether they were specifically interested in businesses under my family's domain or not, she wasn't involved in their investigations. She showed no sign of suspecting there were any deep-seated problems in the city that she'd consider tackling. That night when I'd seen her at the dance club must have been just a fun outing for her, not any kind of work.

Which meant that technically there wasn't any good reason for me to continue spending time with her. Not from a business perspective, anyway.

From a personal perspective... If she wasn't entangled in anything that clashed with my other interests, then there was no reason I shouldn't see her again for my own happiness, was there? I was allowed a little time off from worrying about the business now and then.

And this woman made me think that devoting the time to her would be more than worthwhile.

Maddie scooped the last of her rice into her mouth, and the server came by with the bill. I grabbed it before Maddie could and took out my wallet.

"We should split it," she protested.

I gave her an amused look. "Of course you'd say

that. I'm not going to tell you that men should always pay for women, because I know you think that's bull. And it is. Some of the most capable people I've ever met are women. But my personal stance is that the person who does the inviting does the paying. Can you give me that?"

Maddie narrowed her eyes at me, but a smile touched her lips at the same time. It turned slyer before she spoke. "Then I'll just have to invite you someplace and pay for you next."

She was openly talking about us getting together again before the date was even over. I'd call that a win. The flicker of joy it sent through me was more potent than it probably should be, but what the hell.

It'd been quite a while since I'd gotten to hang out with someone who could make me smile like she did.

"I look forward to hearing your plans," I said, grinning back at her with honest enthusiasm.

After the server brought back my card, we walked out to where Maddie had parked her car. She stopped on the sidewalk by the driver's seat and turned toward me. A faint flush had colored her cheeks that only made her look more delicious.

Fuck caution. I was a man who went after what he wanted. I touched her cheek, and when she shifted toward me as if drawn by a magnet, I captured her mouth in a kiss.

She kissed me back, her lips melding with mine eagerly enough to send a wave of sparks over my skin. Her floral scent filled my lungs, and suddenly all I wanted to do was to lift her up on the hood of the car, strip the pants right off her, and show her just how good I could make her feel. But I wasn't throwing caution to the wind to the point of getting arrested for public indecency.

Besides, Maddie didn't seem like a one-night-stand kind of woman. I didn't want her to think I was only interested in getting her into bed. And she'd already talked about how important her studies were to her—as well as mentioning a project she was working on due later this week.

I eased back, stroking my fingers along her jaw. "I'll let you get back to saving the world," I said in a low voice. "But I definitely want to see you again."

As Maddie beamed at me in response, all I could think of was how much I'd meant that statement. I just hoped I didn't regret how attached I'd already become to the woman in front of me.

CHAPTER
TWENTY

Madelyn

Slade's hands ran down to my waist, hooked around the bottom of my shirt, and moved upward beneath it, his fingers stroking over my smooth skin. I arched into him, my breasts grazing his solid chest. He swept down to capture my mouth, his heat flooding me from head to toe. A needy ache was forming between my legs.

I flung my arms around his neck, and Slade gazed down at me, his dark brown eyes piercing into mine. He lowered himself so the bulge behind his pants grazed my sex, and I rocked my hips to meet him. He kissed my neck, marking a searing path along its slope. One hand slipped under my ass, pressing me tighter against him.

"Slade," I murmured like a plea, and yanked his mouth back to mine. He hugged me close against him as he parted his lips, opening the way for our tongues to tangle together. Oh, God, I wanted—I needed—

"I've got you, Maddie," a familiar voice that wasn't Slade's murmured, even and assured. My fingers slid through tufts of hair that'd turned shorter than Slade's wavy locks.

The man pinning me down wrapped his arm around my waist and flipped us over so I was straddling him, and I found myself looking down into Beckett's gorgeously chiseled features and bright gray eyes. The crisply masculine tang of his cologne filled my nose. I wanted to drink it right off his skin.

He teased his deft hands up my torso to cup my breasts, swiveling his palms over my nipples. The sparks of pleasure made me whimper. Before I knew it, I was grinding against him the way I had Slade. Somehow it all felt perfectly normal, perfectly right. I wanted him too.

I bent down to kiss him, and he growled against my lips with a wildness I didn't remember him showing before. With a powerful surge of his muscles, he hefted me up and carried me across the room to my desk. We were in my dorm, I registered vaguely. Books thumped and pens clattered to the floor as he cleared the way to place me on the desk's top. Then he was kissing me again, devouring me so thoroughly my head spun.

Beckett gripped my hips and pulled me against him. One hand delved between us to work beneath the waist of my pants. Excitement quivered through my core even though some distant part of me wondered if this was a good idea. We'd only kissed once before and now… now…

Now his fingers were gliding right over my clit, and I was crying out against his mouth, and—

The shape of the surface beneath me shifted, and so did the man in front of me. Logan's taller, brawnier form loomed as he braced me against the sink in the basement bathroom back home. His head bowed toward mine, his eyes glinting with a golden sheen full of heated longing.

"Maddie," he muttered. He'd just rolled the condom over his shaft, the head nudging between my thighs where my pants had vanished. The ache inside me swelled, and I clamped my legs around his hips.

"Please," I said, and he plunged into me at the same moment as he claimed my mouth with his. He was all around me with his raw, musky scent, filling me and plundering me, and I wanted nothing more than to buck against him until we both—

My leg kicked to the side and hit thick cloth. Something was tangled all around me—I was on my back again, but there was only a light warmth covering me, no masculine heat.

I blinked, and reality came rushing in. I was lying in my dorm-room bed, totally alone, sweat dampening my skin. It'd been a dream. A way-too-realistic dream. My pussy was throbbing as if those three men really had brought me to the brink of release.

Oh, crap, had any of the noises I'd been making carried through to reality? My gaze shot to the bed opposite mine, and I saw with a rush of relief that Keeley had already left. It was just me in the room with my hormones racing through me on overdrive.

I sat up, rubbed my face, and gathered my clothes to take a shower. But even after several minutes under the spray, which I turned as cold as I could stand it to wash away the lingering horniness, the memory of the dream still brought a flush to my cheeks.

Back in the dorm room, I picked up my phone and typed out a text to Summer. *Had a crazy dream. You know how I told you that I've gotten kind of close with one of Logan's friends, Slade? I was making out all hot and heavy with him, and then it was Beckett I was all over, and then I was back at home that night with Logan… Am I totally insane? Who lusts after three guys in the space of five minutes?*

As I packed my bag for my morning classes, the phone chimed with Summer's answer. *Logan can GTFO, but I see no problems with getting it on with two hot guys who seem into you. Why shouldn't you enjoy both of them, in your imagination… or in reality too? ;) Let them remind you what you're worth, since that jackass doesn't have a clue.*

I shouldn't have been surprised. My mouth twitched with a smile. Maybe she was right. College was supposed to be the time for casual hookups and experimenting, even if that wasn't my typical approach. If both of the guys wanted me, and I wanted them… I'd make sure they knew I wasn't exclusive, but there wasn't anything wrong with me seeing where things could go with both of them.

It really shouldn't have been so hard for me to believe that two hot guys *could* want me. I guessed I could thank Logan for that, at least partly.

I paused after zipping up my bag and swallowed hard. Our encounter—and the way he'd ghosted me afterward —had cast a long shadow over my dating life. Somehow I'd spent more time with him in the past week than I had in years, and we'd barely touched on the one event that had altered our relationship irrevocably while also sending him running. Even when I'd tried to confront him before, I'd danced around the subject, unsure of how to address it.

We'd had something once, I knew that—even if it'd only been friendship for most of that time. A piece of my heart was still drawn to him, longing to understand him… I didn't think I could give myself over to pursuing more with any other guy until the air was totally clear between us. There'd always be a lingering "what if" in the back of my head.

He owed me a proper explanation anyway, no matter how much he'd resisted before. If it was a shitty explanation, well, that'd tell me all I needed to know and make it that much easier to move on.

I'd be seeing him tonight. We were supposed to be checking out a bar on the outskirts of downtown. Dexter had turned up an old bill at Melinda Hughes's house that'd been in a man's name, a man the Vigil guys had determined was the manager at that bar. He could be the one who owned the car Logan had heard about, using her address for that too.

But I didn't want to have a conversation like this in front of the other guys. There was no way Logan would open up with his friends within hearing. I wasn't even sure if they knew we'd hooked up.

No, this was better kept private, just between us.

In between classes, I did my readings on a bench within view of the law library entrance, enjoying the spring sunlight and the warmth it cast over me. It wasn't until the early afternoon when I spotted Logan's tall form striding toward the library.

I hadn't seen any of the other guys go in. Hopefully I'd be able to catch him alone in there. I stuffed my book into my bag, swung it over my shoulder, and hurried after him.

The door to the Vigil office hadn't completely closed, the latch just slightly ajar. I pulled it open and found Logan sitting on the edge of the computer desk, shuffling a deck of cards. That was strange enough that my eyes darted to the images on the cards, and I realized it was even odder than I'd initially thought. They weren't playing cards but tarot cards by the look of them.

"What are those for?" I blurted out as Logan's head jerked up at my entrance.

He frowned at me, his hands stilling. Nudging the cards into a straight formation, he slid them into the box that'd been sitting on the desk next to him and then shoved that into the desk's drawer. "Just a tool for inspiration. Nothing important. What are you doing here? We're not heading out until tonight, when the bar'll be open and busy."

Shit. I'd already put him on the defensive. I groped for a way to smooth over the situation and decided there really wasn't any. Honestly, even if I hadn't asked an abrupt question, Logan seemed to take offense to just about everything I said these days.

"I needed to talk to you," I said instead, figuring it was best to get straight to the point. "Just you."

Logan's stance had already tensed when I'd come in, but now his shoulders went slightly more rigid. He narrowed his eyes at me. "About what?" he asked flatly. "I thought we were all talked out after our last private chat."

I drew myself up straighter, girding myself. I would not let him intimidate me out of this. I wouldn't let him make me feel small or pathetic. Something was going on—something *had* been going on two years ago—and I had a right to know why it'd screwed things up between us so epically.

I tugged the door all the way shut and leaned against the doorframe, crossing my arms over my chest. "I've held my own with you and the other guys through every part of this investigation so far. I think I've proven that I'm not weak anymore like I was back in junior high when you had to jump in to defend me. I can *defend* myself now. You don't have to worry about what I can or can't handle."

Logan's expression gave away nothing. His bright

brown eyes, which had shone so hungrily in my dream, held only impatience. "Fine. You're a strong, independent woman. I get it. Is there a point to this or did you just want my approval?"

God, did he always have to needle me in just the right way to get under my skin? My jaw clenched, but I forced it to relax.

"I need you to tell me what happened the night we hooked up," I said, keeping my own voice as calm as possible. "I *know* something was up. I've seen the kind of things you've been doing now. Why were you all banged up? Were you investigating something all the way back in our town—something people were willing to fight you over?"

I'd thought Logan had looked obstinate before, but now his demeanor turned absolutely impenetrable. "That's none of your business."

I pushed myself off the doorframe and took a step toward him. "No, I think it is my business. I was there with you then, and I'm here now. I need to understand. You didn't want me to know what you'd been doing. And then, after— You can't tell me that you shut me out and blocked me everywhere because you assumed I'd be clingy or something. *You* were just as into it as I was. You kissed me first. And I was already giving you nothing but space up until that night. So there's got to be something else, maybe something you're keeping me out of—"

"For fuck's sake, Madelyn," Logan broke in, his tone gone harsh. "Not everything is about you. We hooked up, we both got off, and that's the end of it. It didn't mean anything, and it doesn't have anything to do with anything else in my life. I'm not interested in talking about anything to do with that night, especially the part you were involved in. Because you know what? I try not to think about it at all."

His words and the way he spat them at me hit me like a slap to the face. Shame washed over me, but with it came a surge of anger that he was making me feel ashamed for what I'd said. For letting that night have any importance at all.

Why should I even bother finding out what was going on if this was how he wanted things to be? Why was I wasting any more energy on this jerk than I already had? Nothing I'd done in the past week had made a speck of difference to him.

"You know what?" I snapped back, my patience frayed. "You should consider yourself lucky that I've cared as much about how *you* feel about things as I do. I gave you two years to get your head out of your ass and apologize for *being* such an ass, or at least give me something resembling an explanation. I've done nothing but keep out of your way until now. So forgive me for thinking you might treat me with even as much respect as you'd give some stranger you don't even know."

I spun around and shoved past the door. My feet didn't stop moving until I'd put the law library far behind me. I stalled at the edge of the path, a tremble running through my body, and rubbed my hands over my face.

I hadn't meant to lose my temper. But... we'd shared something, whether Logan wanted to admit it or not. Either that, or he'd sure as hell pretended to be affected by our hookup while it was happening. The things he'd said... He'd had no reason to lie if he'd planned on ghosting me right after.

He wasn't interested in me that way now, and that was fine, but he had no excuse for being so hostile. Unless he was hiding something. But why couldn't he trust me even a tiny bit after everything we'd been through just this week?

I glanced across the lawn toward the parking lot outside my dorm, which I'd stormed toward without really thinking about it. My gaze settled on my car—the car we'd worked together to recover. An unexpected sense of resolve rose up inside me.

I set off toward the car, my hands balling at my sides. I was going to prove to him once and for all that I was his equal, not some useless, clingy girl. And if he still didn't want to see it, at least I'd have proven it definitively to myself. He could go drown in his troubles for all I cared, but I'd look after what mattered to me for myself.

CHAPTER
TWENTY-ONE

Madelyn

I parked down the street from the bar, grateful that Dexter had mentioned its name when he'd contacted me to let me know about tonight's plans. That meant I'd been able to look up the address.

For a few minutes, I just studied the outside of the building from down the street. It was a plain if scruffy brick building, distinguished by the bright orange door and the silver lettering that stood out against the large black sign overhead. No one came in or out while I watched, but that wasn't surprising. My internet search had also told me that the place didn't open until five o'clock, a couple of hours from now.

The guys had planned on scoping the place out like regular customers, but I couldn't help thinking I'd be more likely to find evidence of illegal dealings while the clientele wasn't around. Maybe if they hadn't felt obligated to bring me along, they'd have broken in like they had the house the other day. But even the three of them going in together made it more likely they'd get caught.

I couldn't pick locks, but if I could spot something from the outside or even find my way in and dig up a clue, no one would be able to claim I couldn't hold my own alongside them. I'd have done something they hadn't managed to, all on my own.

My heart thumped at a brisk beat, but I willed my nerves to settle down. This was no big deal. Logan and the others pulled crap like this all the time. It could be just an ordinary bar—the only thing we knew about it was that the manager had used Melinda Hughes as some kind of front address. Which, okay, suggested he might not be totally on the up-and-up, but it didn't necessarily make him outright dangerous.

And there shouldn't be much of anyone around the place this long before opening anyway.

Gathering my courage, I stepped out of the car. Figuring it was better to do this with as little baggage as possible, I left my purse behind and simply stuffed my phone in my pocket in case I needed to take on Dexter's role as evidence photographer. Then I ambled down the street toward the bar at as casual a pace as I could manage.

I passed a café where patrons were chattering to each other behind the front window and a couple of shops with a few customers browsing inside. No one stirred around the bar. The front door would obviously be locked, and I'd look strange if anyone saw me trying it. I simply meandered on by the front of the building, eyeing the window surreptitiously.

The main room was cast in shadows, but I made out several square tables, all dark wood, and a wide wooden bar counter toward the back of the space. There was no one inside at the moment. Perfect.

A narrow lane on the far side of the bar led around behind the building. I ducked down it and picked up my pace, the back of my neck prickling. Thankfully, I had the foresight to set my feet quietly, because I was just a few steps down when I heard the scrape of something moving around the back.

I slowed down again and crept the rest of the way to the corner of the wall. There, I peeked around the building.

The lane connected to a wider alley that ran down the middle of the block past the backs of all the buildings. A truck was parked outside the bar, the back end open, boxes stacked inside it. Several of them had logos I recognized—they were cases of alcohol. Well, there wasn't anything particularly suspicious about a bar getting a booze delivery.

More interesting to me was the door that'd been propped open with a wedge underneath it. A guy who didn't look much older than me strode out and grabbed another case. A rhythmic hiss of music carried from the headphones he wore, which must have been blaring. He carried the case inside, leaving the door wide open.

My mouth went dry. This was my chance. I could

get inside and poke around, as long as that one employee didn't catch me. I should be able to manage that, right? The guy definitely wasn't in a position to hear anything outside his headphones. As long as he didn't see me, I was golden.

I couldn't let the opportunity pass me by when luck was working in my favor.

I darted toward the back door, listening carefully for the seeping music. There was no sound in the dark hall on the other side. I slipped inside, my heart racing, and caught the sound of footsteps coming from a doorway to my right. I dashed in the opposite direction, to a door a little farther down on the left.

It was a kitchen, dim and dingy with a greasy smell lingering in the air. I didn't think this place served up fine cuisine.

Moving as quietly and quickly as I could, I slunk through the cramped space. I peeked into the cupboards and drawers, scanned the countertops and beneath the cabinets, and studied every object that came into view. I *had* to find some piece of evidence to bring back to Logan, whether it proved that the bar had nothing to do with the case or that the culprits worked here. The thought of his sneering dismissal brought a rush of anger back to the surface.

He was going to see that I wasn't some helpless kitten in need of protection, incapable of understanding whatever the hell he'd been through in the last few years. That I was just as resilient as he was, and putting me down wasn't going to stop me from getting what I wanted.

Unfortunately, the kitchen offered nothing remotely useful one way or the other. I paused with a grimace and poked my head into the hallway.

The guy was just stepping outside again. The moment he'd passed out of view, I hustled across the hall to another doorway just before the main room.

It proved to be a storage room, about the size of a janitor's closet—and true to form, it mostly held cleaning supplies. I shifted the various objects on the shelves around, finding rolls of receipt paper for the cash register, blank order slips, and a box of pens as well, but none of that was any help.

The manager must have some kind of office, right? A private area where he handled any business to do with the bar. Where was that?

I slipped out into the main bar room. The place was packed with tables, barely enough room for neighboring chairs to be pulled out at the same time. The ones near the front were all the square four-seaters I'd seen from the window; a few eight-person round tables stood closer to the back, near the bar.

The bar itself ran in an L-shape with the long end next to me along the back wall and a smaller bit jutting out at the far side, holding the cash register. Just beyond the register, I spotted another door. A tarnished brass plaque mounted on it said simply MANAGER. Bingo.

I checked the back of the bar on my way to the office, giving the shelves beneath the counter and along the wall a quick skim. Everything looked like standard bar equipment, as far as I could tell. A clipboard had been tucked away on one shelf, but all I found on the one sheet that had writing on it was a list of drink ingredients, maybe something custom a patron had asked for.

As I set it down and straightened up, my gaze caught on a folded paper left on one of the circular tables near the end of the bar. That must be something an employee had left there, right, since everything from last night's customers would have been cleaned up? I dashed over to check it out.

To my dismay, I found only a crude doodle of a guy waving his gigantic dick. Rolling my eyes, I set it down —just as a click rang through the room with the turning of the knob on the manager's office door.

My stomach lurched. I threw myself down into a crouch beneath the level of the table, squeezing between the chairs on either side of me.

Thank God I hadn't continued straight to that door and opened it myself. Three men and a woman sauntered out of the office, muttering to each other, one letting out a dark chuckle. All of them moved with obvious strength, twisted tattoos winding across one man's neck and the woman's arms, another man sporting a scar stretching across his cheek to his jaw.

The woman ran her hand through her spiky pixie cut, which was a flat black color I had to assume was dyed, and her leather jacket rode up enough for me to spot the handle of a pistol tucked in the back of her jeans. One of the men lifted his hand, and I realized he was outright holding a gun himself. My breath snagged in my throat.

Okay, these people were definitely dangerous. Shit. What the hell had I gotten myself into?

The four figures had gathered around the bar, one of them going behind to grab a bottle I couldn't make out the label on. It took several more seconds before my panic evened out enough for me to pay attention to the conversation they were having in aggressive tones that only set me more on edge.

"Pop a cap in all of them. It's the most effective way to stop their shit," the man with the bottle said in a deep, angry voice as he poured the alcohol into a couple of glasses.

The guy with the gun snatched one of the glasses and let out a sigh of frustration. "We've got to catch the pricks first. Their staff don't know shit about this."

"We can't let them get away with it," the third guy said. "A little rivalry is fine, but when they stoop to the level of vandalizing our property? Fuck that. They're all a bunch of low-life scumbags anyway. We'd be doing the city a service getting rid of the fuckers."

"No kidding," the woman said in a guttural voice, and made a grabby gesture toward the bottle. "You going to pour some of that for me?"

They were definitely criminals, but there was no reason to think that they had anything to do with my car or Dad's box from what they'd said so far. I held the rest of my body perfectly still while my head swiveled, considering possible escape routes.

The conclusion crept over me with a sinking sensation in my gut that I was screwed unless the group at the bar left before anyone came in the front where they could spot me under the table. I couldn't make a run for the front door without those four noticing me; same story with the back hall. The tables might be close together, but that only worked against me. If I tried to squeeze around them toward the hall, I'd end up brushing against a chair and drawing attention to myself.

Maybe this bunch would leave after they'd had their drink and hashed out their problem a little more? Surely they weren't going to hang out there all the way until opening time.

"Marvin's right," the first man was saying. "They attacked us, and we have to retaliate. Otherwise we're just inviting them to screw us over again."

"Can't be anything too blatant," the second guy said. "We don't want the police getting all up in our shit."

The glasses clinked, and then one of the pairs of legs moved toward my table. My hunched stance went even more rigid. I stared at the jean-clad legs and the scuffed leather boots beneath them, willing them to stop, to head somewhere else.

The man did stop, but right at the edge of the table next to mine. If he came much farther around it and looked down, he'd see me for sure. He set his glass down on the table and drummed his fingers against the surface, each tap reverberating alongside my thudding heart.

This was bad. Really bad. Every particle in my body balked against the realization rising up in me, but I couldn't deny it.

I'd gotten myself into a horrible jam, and I was going to need help if I wanted to have a decent chance of getting out of it unharmed. What was more important, my pride or ensuring these people didn't "pop a cap" in *me*?

If Logan never let me live it down, well… I guessed I'd have to back out of any further parts of the investigation. A flush that was part frustration, part shame prickled over my face, but my panic blared far louder.

I didn't want to *die*. Fighting off a single unarmed thug was one thing. Taking on four criminals, at least two of whom had guns… I wasn't a superhero. I could admit I'd gotten out of my depth.

Breathing softly and shallowly, I eased my hand over to my pocket. Ever so carefully, I slid out my phone. My hand shook, but the guy at the nearby table was focused on his companions, grumbling about trashing somebody's home. I still had a little time before I was discovered.

The name at the top of my recent text threads was Dexter. Well, he was the most reliable out of the three guys anyway. I certainly couldn't call on anyone outside the Vigil to extricate me from this ridiculous mess. The thought of trying to explain to Keeley what was going on made me shiver. And I could hardly call the police when technically *I* was the only one who'd done anything illegal here, sneaking into a building where I had no permission to be.

I set the phone on silent, typed out a shaky message as quickly as I could with my trembling fingers, hit send, and slid the device back into my pocket. Please, let them get here fast. Let them know how to create some kind of distraction so that I could get out of here.

Just let them come. They had to come, or I was the one who'd be screwed.

CHAPTER
TWENTY-TWO

Slade

"I knew we should never have let her get involved in the first place," Logan growled, his knuckles white where he was gripping the steering wheel. "Going in there on her own like that—so fucking stupid. Reckless and stupid."

The engine roared as he hurtled through the streets, cutting off other cars and speeding through stoplights that were seconds from turning red. If I hadn't been in the car with him during similar high-speed drives, I'd have been clutching the handle for dear life. As it was, my pulse thumped heavily with a combination of anxiety and my own frustration.

Still, I felt the need to defend Maddie. Logan obviously didn't have the most unbiased view of her behavior even at the best of times.

"We've done plenty of things that were even more

stupid than this," I pointed out. "How many situations have we walked into that we knew for sure were dangerous?"

"We weren't even certain that this bar had any criminal affiliations at all," Dexter put in from the back seat.

"It doesn't matter," Logan snapped. "I told her everything we do could be dangerous. She's seen the kind of people we've run into investigating the theft. Does she have a death wish or something?"

I suspected the people most likely to die in this scenario were anyone who got in between Logan and Maddie, whatever we had to do to drag her out of the place. He was so worked up a vein was bulging at his temple. I wasn't sure I'd *ever* seen him this pissed off.

How much of it was because of Maddie defying him, and how much because he was worried about her safety just like I was? He could deny he had any interest in her all he wanted, but he clearly cared, one way or another.

"You kept trying to convince her that she couldn't handle running around with us at all," I said, keeping my tone light. "Apparently that only made her more determined to prove herself. Maybe that's a hint that you should change your tactics."

Logan's next growl was a wordless sound of fury. I decided I'd better drop the subject there.

Besides, my insides were so tangled up with tension that it was hard to keep the breezy tone I'd been going for. It'd already been twenty minutes since Dexter had gotten the text and alerted us. Even at the speed Logan was driving, the bar was at least another ten minutes away. What if the people Maddie had been worried about had caught her? What would they do to her if they did?

It was hard to know how worried I needed to be, but she'd mentioned they had guns. It didn't sound like they were just regular bar staff having a casual pre-opening chat.

"Have you heard anything else from her?" I couldn't help asking, glancing back at Dexter.

He shook his head, his mouth tight. Even he was worried from his intensely practical perspective. Shit.

"It's better that she doesn't do anything else that could draw attention to her presence," he said, but that fact didn't give me much comfort.

A weird twinge of what I had to admit was jealousy rippled through my panic. Maddie had my number too. I hadn't seen her talking to Dexter other than brief discussions about the case. Why had she reached out to him for help instead of me?

Maybe she hadn't figured I'd be as reliable as him? I didn't exactly present myself as Mr. Responsibility.

But I wanted to be that kind of guy for her. The more time we spent together, the more I couldn't wait to see her again. And she'd shown when we were making out in the house the other day that she saw me as more than a meaningless good time. How many girls had looked at me as more than a brief, fun fling, not caring whether I was at all invested in them?

I had to prove that I was worth that kind of consideration. Worthy of being someone she "actually liked" and didn't just want to goof around with. I should be a guy she could turn to at least as much as she could trust Dexter with that role.

But I'd never been that guy for anyone before. I wasn't totally sure how to be. Fuck.

I guessed getting her out of this jam would be a good step in the right direction, anyway. If we could pull that off.

I squinted at the road ahead. My foot tapped restlessly against the floor. I popped one of my cinnamon candies into my mouth for something to do and immediately regretted it. It reminded me of kissing Maddie... and when Logan threw the car around a corner, I almost choked on it.

"It doesn't make sense that she'd go off and do this right now, though." I frowned. "We let her be totally involved when we broke into the house. She seemed satisfied with that, and we'd already looped her in on the trip to the bar tonight. Why would she suddenly decide that she had to get in there early when nothing changed?"

Dexter hummed in the back seat. "It is strange, and not consistent with how she's acted so far. But maybe something did happen that we don't know about that made her feel the situation was more urgent?"

"Or maybe she's a clueless ditz who makes idiotic decisions," Logan snarled, but he didn't sound as emphatic about that suggestion as in his earlier complaints.

I glanced at him, one eyebrow rising as suspicion gripped me. "Did *you* talk to her earlier today? Did you get all grouchy about her being involved again? That could have set her off."

"I didn't say anything to her about the investigation," Logan shot back. "I sure as hell didn't give any impression that going into the bar early was a good idea."

I could read into what he didn't say well enough, especially with the tick of his jaw before he clenched it. "But you did talk to her. For fuck's sake. What *did* you say?"

The tires squealed as he was forced to brake at a stoplight. He turned his head to glare at me. "Nothing that's any justification for her going off like this, trying to get herself killed."

Normally I wouldn't have challenged my best friend. I trusted him, I had his back, and I knew that loyalty went both ways. But it seemed to me that part of having his back was standing up to him when he was being a prick over a woman who didn't deserve it. I could do that for Maddie even if she wasn't here to see me defend her.

I didn't want to make him more furious, though, not when we needed him thinking at least somewhat clearly to confront the assholes who had Maddie cornered. So I just gazed steadily back at him and said in an even tone, "Maybe after we get her out of that hellhole, you should think a little harder about that. Because I haven't seen her do anything so far that wasn't justified."

Logan jerked his eyes back to the road with the change of the light and hit the gas. He drove on in stormy silence that I decided it was better not to break. I tried to picture how we'd arrange to get Maddie safely out of the bar, but it was hard to come up with a plan when we hadn't scoped the place out yet—and planning wasn't exactly my specialty anyway.

We tore around another bend, and then Logan slowed. I recognized Maddie's car a block up ahead by the side of the road. "She was smart enough not to park right out front," I remarked.

Logan just snorted. He pulled in behind it, moving in brusque jerks.

"If her car's still here, then she's still inside," Dexter remarked as we got out, and then shook his head at himself with a rustle of his messy curls. "Of course, if she'd gotten out I'm sure she'd have texted us to let us know."

"Let's get going then," I said, bouncing on my feet.

Logan took a deep breath as if to steady himself. His jaw was still clenched, his hands in fists, but he still knew how to be a leader.

"We'll take a quick look around to see what we're dealing with," he said. "We could screw things up more if we go barging in unprepared. Keep your eyes peeled, and move *fast*."

We had no idea how much trouble Maddie was

already in. My stomach twisted as we hustled down the street together. I picked out the bar up ahead with the glinting lettering on its otherwise black sign. Then, as we drew closer, my gaze snagged on something that made my spirits sink even farther.

I pointed to the black shape spray-painted on the dark brick at the corner of the wall. "There's a gang sign. Looks like it's been there for a while and repainted. Isn't that the sign for those assholes we tangled with last year when we were helping that kid whose mom was being shaken down."

"Shit," Logan said through clenched teeth. By now, we all knew how to tell when a gang had claimed a particular property as their own, which meant they had at least some say in the operations. If Maddie had seen armed men inside, this was probably one of their business fronts. And these lowlifes seemed to be one of the bigger gangs in town, definitely one of the most vicious. I had a scar on my bicep from when one of the assholes had come at me with a knife, even though all we'd been doing was asking a few questions.

I'd hoped we'd get to steer clear of them after that. No such luck. Their criminal affiliations made it even more likely that they were involved in the car theft and whatever had gone down with Maddie's father's box… and even more likely that she'd be in deep shit if they caught her having snuck into their hangout.

Neither of the other guys showed any indication that they were second-guessing our rescue attempt. Logan's eyes had narrowed in concentration. "We'll go in, but we need to keep it looking casual. Play it off like we're trying to help somehow, not a threat. Maybe we can stop any shots from being fired. All she needs is a distraction so she can make a run for the exit."

All she needs. As if it were that simple. I squared my shoulders and marched with the other guys the rest of the way to the bar, pasting a smile on my face but inwardly preparing to do battle.

Whatever she needed, whatever lengths we had to go to, we were getting her out of this mess.

CHAPTER
TWENTY-THREE

Madelyn

stayed crouched beneath the table until my calves
started to ache from holding so still, waiting while
the four apparent gangsters hashed out how they
were going to take revenge on what I was gathering were
the criminals running a rival bar.

Were the Vigil guys even coming? How long would
it take them to get here even if they were?

The man who'd walked closer to my table
meandered around a bit, making my pulse stutter
several times. Then the whole group ambled over to a
table at the far side of the room from me. They sat
down with their backs to me, mostly facing the front
door.

My heart skipped in a different way. Maybe I could
get out of this on my own after all. It was only a short

distance from my hiding spot to the end of the bar where the cash register sat. If I could creep around behind the bar and make the short dash to the back hall without being spotted…

I eased out from between the chairs inch by inch and crawled around them toward the short end of the bar's L shape. I had to stop and twist to squeeze past another table, but then I was able to shuffle the last couple of steps to the shelter of the bar counter.

Slumping behind it, a breath rushed out of me. The gangsters were still talking away, their aggressive voices interspersed with harsh chuckles. They weren't at all suspicious—none of them had any clue I was in the room. Now I just had to make it to the hall.

I was just creeping around the corner of the bar when another man strode into the room from the back, the way I'd originally come. As I jerked back out of view, almost choking on my tongue, I recognized him as the guy who'd been unloading the delivery truck. His headphones were looped around his neck now.

He stopped just outside the hall. "Everything came other than they sent a replacement for the one brand of vodka you wanted—the Belvedere. The replacement stuff looks like similar quality, though."

One of the men at the table let out a huff. "They're supposed to call before making any substitutions. Fuckers."

"Do you want me to load it back in and hassle them about it?"

"Nah, it's here now. But I'll make sure they know not to pull that shit again. Hey, is that friend of yours still collecting bets on tonight's game?"

I gritted my teeth in impatient silence as their conversation dragged on. The guy was blocking my escape route. What was I supposed to do now?

I guessed while I was waiting for him to leave again, I might as well take a closer look at what was stashed under the cash register. Maybe I'd missed something.

I peered at the shelves, shifting aside the few papers I could move without making much noise. Nothing jumped out at me as particularly useful. Some receipts were tucked way at the back, but they looked totally normal—they definitely didn't have anything to do with my car or Dad's box.

A tablet was tucked away at the back of the lowest shelf. I slid it out and tried to turn it on, but naturally it asked for a passcode. I wasn't going to be able to come up with that. Making a face at it, I shoved it back into place.

My gaze lifted toward the cash register and caught on a thin rectangular shape next to it at the edge of the counter. A phone. Someone from the group must have left it there while they were getting drinks. What information might be on *that*?

I wavered, wondering if it was worth the risk of trying to grab it. If I snatched it and could get out of here, they wouldn't realize right away that it'd been stolen. They'd probably just assume it'd been misplaced, considering that as far as they knew, no one else had been in here.

Or was that just wishful thinking?

I bit my lip and was on the verge of reaching for it when a text alert chimed from the device, pealing through the room.

I clamped my mouth shut against a yelp and jerked back down. One of the men muttered a curse, and footsteps thumped toward me. My heartbeat thundered in my ears as he approached. What if he looked over the top of the bar and saw me?

There was nowhere for me to go where I wouldn't be even more easily seen. I pressed myself against the base of the bar counter as tightly as I could, holding my breath. He had no reason to check behind the bar. As long as I stayed totally still and quiet…

The footsteps stopped. I didn't even dare look up. My stomach lurched queasily.

And then the man lifted his phone off the counter with a faint rasp and walked away again without any sign of concern.

"George," he muttered to the others. "Can't that guy handle anything on his own?"

The woman snorted. "From what I've seen, nope, not at all."

Okay. I'd survived another close call. As my pulse started to even out again, I peeked around the corner of the bar toward the hall—but the guy with the headphones was still standing there, laughing at another comment one of his colleagues had made about this George person. Why wouldn't he just move?

Staring daggers at him didn't accomplish anything. Swallowing a sigh, I swiveled around—and realized that the door to the manager's office, just a few feet away from me, had been left ajar when the group had marched out into the main room.

I'd wanted to take a look in there. Maybe it wasn't worth the risk of trying to sneak right inside while there were so many employees around, but I could at least check out what I could glimpse from the doorway. It wasn't as if I had anything else to do at the moment.

If I could come out of this mess with just one useful piece of information, that would make the humiliation I was going to face when the Vigil guys got here worth it.

I crept closer, past a couple of rows of empty liquor bottles that'd been left against the wall behind the bar. I had to move a little beyond the shelter of the counter, but while I was crouched this low, the tables still hid me from everyone else in the room. I craned my neck to peer into the office.

There was a filing cabinet directly across from me with a signed baseball and a football helmet poised on it. I guessed the manager was a sports fan. Over to the side, I could make out the edge of a desk, a few papers scattered across its surface and a glass ringed with amber liquid holding a couple of them down. I leaned forward a little farther to take in more of the desk and lost my breath all over again.

It was there. A familiar black lacquer box, the glint of the silver Celtic knot just barely visible on the top, sitting off to the side of the desk at a haphazard angle as if someone had casually tossed it there.

Not only were these people connected to the theft of my car, but the manager himself must have wanted Dad's box for some reason.

Exhilaration rushed through me. I'd found it. Maybe I couldn't poke around the whole office, but could I get away with nudging the door a little farther open and slipping inside just long enough to grab it? I could have Dad's prized possession back in my grasp and prove to the Vigil guys that my expedition here hadn't been totally useless.

I edged slightly closer, running my fingers lightly along the door, testing how easy it'd be to push it. I didn't get much sense of resistance. I hadn't heard the hinges squeak when it'd opened before. The group at the table were still facing away from here. If I moved it slowly enough, smidge by smidge…

I was just about to make that first push when a chair squeaked and a figure loomed in the gap between the door and the frame. It was a man, walking past the doorway to reach for the filing cabinet. The office wasn't empty after all.

The jolt of startled panic sent me jerking a step backward—and my heel collided with one of the lined-up bottles. It clicked against the others and toppled over with a *thunk* that seemed to echo through the room. My heart outright stopped.

"What the fuck was that?" one of the men at the table demanded, with a squeak of his chair's legs as he got to his feet. I froze in place, knowing it was only a matter of seconds before he and his friends with their guns descended on me.

What the hell did I do now?

CHAPTER
TWENTY-FOUR

Madelyn

Multiple sets of footsteps rapped across the floor toward the bar. A shuffling sound from within the office told me the man there was turning toward the door too. With a stutter of my pulse, I pushed myself farther behind the counter even though I knew that effort was in vain.

They were going to take a closer look around this time. They were going to search for whatever had made that noise, and it would lead them straight to me. And my way to both possible escape routes was still blocked. Shit.

"Hey, is someone there?" the woman called out, sounding like she was right on the other side of the counter. I balled my hands into fists, my mind scrambling for an excuse that might get me out of this safely—

A loud banging sounded from the front of the building, someone knocking on the door hard enough that it rattled in its frame. Shoes scraped against the floor as the nearby figures must have swiveled.

"What the fuck do they want?" one of the men muttered. "The CLOSED sign is hanging right there."

Voices started to filter through the door.

"Hey! Open up."

"We've got to talk to you. This is important."

That sounded like Slade and Logan. My heart skipped a beat. They'd made it here just in time. But what kind of distraction were they making? I didn't want them getting into trouble with these gangsters because of me.

I hoped they knew what they were doing—and that it'd be enough to give me a chance to escape.

To my relief, all of the footsteps moved away from me. The guy who'd been in the office emerged, visible around the edge of the bar, but he didn't glance my way, all his attention focused on the front of the room. "What's going on?"

"Looks like some college guys making a fuss," one of the men reported from near the door. "I'll see what they're going on about."

There was the click of the door unlocking and a faint squeak of the hinges. "What the hell do you want?" he demanded.

My gaze flicked back and forth, noting that the man from the manager's office was still standing near that doorway and the guy who'd handled the delivery hadn't moved far from the back hall. I still couldn't make a dash for the back exit without being seen.

Logan's voice carried through the room, both bold and urgent. "We overheard some scummy-looking guys a few blocks away talking about how they were going to come here and smash up your bar. I don't know how soon, but they sounded serious. We couldn't just let them go ahead with it without warning you."

For the first time since I'd gotten stuck in here, a smile darted across my lips. He had no idea how perfect that story was given the concerns these gangsters already had about their property—or maybe he did. For all I knew, the Vigil guys were perfectly familiar with the kinds of criminal conflicts going on around the city. Even if they hadn't known anything about the people who owned this specific bar, it might not be hard to figure out what kind of news would get them riled up.

"Are you serious?" the man by the door demanded. "What else did they say?"

Slade spoke next. "We didn't really want to stick around to eavesdrop on guys who'd do shit like that. It sounded like they were pissed off about a deal or something? I don't know what they meant."

Both of the men I'd still been able to see stepped completely out of my view, moving toward the front door to join the conversation. From the sounds of the feet beyond the bar counter, everyone was gathering around the door to talk to the Vigil guys.

Relief flooded me. I'd just give them time to get

fully engaged in the conversation, and then I could dash for the back.

"What exactly did you hear?" another of the men asked in a firm voice that suggested he had some authority over the others. "Word for word, as well as you can remember."

As Logan continued to spin his story, I glanced around again, and my gaze snagged on the now wide-open door to the manager's office. I could see Dad's lacquer box from where I was crouched. The sight of it tugged at my chest.

I squared my shoulders. I wasn't coming out of this empty-handed. They'd taken something important from me, and I was taking it right back while I had the chance.

I scrambled over to the end of the bar and peeked around the counter. The six figures were now clustered around the door, all of them focused on the Vigil guys. This was the best opportunity I was going to get. Grab the box, then get the hell out of here.

With a swift breath, I darted across the short open space and through the office doorway. My eyes swept over the contents of the office with a pang as I thought of all the other evidence that might be in here, all the answers we might be able to find about why these people had taken Dad's box in the first place, but there was no time to do a more thorough search. Even this quick maneuver was risky—and it wasn't just *my* safety on the line now.

I snatched the box off the desk, tucked it under my

arm, and hustled back into the shelter of the bar beneath the level of the nearest table. As quickly as I could while ducked down, I scuttled to the opposite end of the counter near the back hall. The guys were still talking, but their voices were muffled by the thudding of my pulse.

I was just lunging into the shadows of the hall when one comment reached my ears that made my stomach flip over.

"Wait. You look kind of familiar. Weren't you and your friends making some kind of trouble for our guys downtown a while back?"

The tone got more menacing with each word. My throat tightened at the thought that the guys might be able to face some horrible consequence, but they should be able to leave now. Hopefully they'd been able to see me head this way. I pushed myself forward, my gaze fixed on the back door.

Which swung open to admit a stout burly guy I hadn't seen before.

He took one look at me, and his face twisted with anger and suspicion. "Who the hell are you, and what are you doing back here?" he bellowed.

"I—" I gasped out, and then he was charging forward, his hands already reaching to grab me.

"What the fuck is going on?" someone shouted from the room behind me, but I didn't have time to worry about that. The fury on the man's face and the muscles bulging in his arms as he threw himself at me sent my instincts honed by my martial arts classes into overdrive.

I dodged to the side and caught him in the throat with an upward swing of my elbow, slamming my knee into his gut at the same time. Despite the choked sound that sputtered from his throat, he locked his hand around my wrist. I kicked out with my leg again and managed to land a blow right between his legs.

As he doubled over, his grip on my arm loosened. I jerked backward, onto the threshold of the main room. Yells and thumps from behind me brought my head jerking around.

The Vigil guys had obviously realized I was under attack, and they'd stormed in to defend me. All of them were beating at the gangsters with vicious intensity, Logan bashing one man in the face hard enough to leave his nose bleeding, Slade cracking another man across the jaw, even quiet, unassuming Dexter kicking a third man's legs out from under him. But they were fighting off the whole group that'd been gathered by the door, outnumbered two to one, and the gangsters weren't backing down or going down easily.

And some of them had guns.

I couldn't fight properly while I was holding on to the box. I set it on the bar counter and rushed over to help.

As all three of the Vigil guys whipped out their fists and hurled their elbows and knees in the middle of the fray, the woman gangster yanked herself back from the bunch and raised her pistol. She aimed it straight at

Logan's head, and he was too busy grappling with one of the bigger guys to notice.

My heart lurched into the base of my throat. I didn't hesitate for a second, just flung myself toward her as quickly as I could move. Chairs clattered and thumped in my wake.

The woman had paused to make sure she had a clear shot without her colleagues getting in the way. When she heard me coming, her head whipped around, but I was already on her by then.

I rammed straight into her and tackled her to the ground. With a smack of my hand, I sent the pistol spinning across the floor. Then I twisted around, squirming to evade her own strikes, and brought my heel down on her fingers as hard as I could.

The sound of fracturing bones sent a wave of nausea through me. The woman screeched. But even as the queasiness coiled around my stomach, a rush of triumph shot through me as well.

I'd protected Logan—saved him. I'd put all my strength into defending the guys and conquering our enemies. And it felt... kind of good.

The woman raked the fingernails of her other hand across my arm, and I pushed away from her, kicking her in the ribs. Then I caught hold of a nearby chair and yanked it down on top of her with enough force to provoke a grunt. I scrambled farther away.

A few of the men had hit the floor under the Vigil guys' assault. Slade grabbed my elbow, heaving me to my feet. "Let's get out of here!"

We raced to the back of the bar, the last two men giving chase. I snatched the box off the counter as we dashed by. The man who'd come at me in the back hall had lurched to his feet, but Logan plowed straight into him, knocking him into one of the storage rooms. We ran on by, ignoring his furious shouts and the bellows from behind us.

The door burst open in our wake. I sprinted around the side of the building and down the street toward my waiting car, aware of all three Vigil guys running alongside me. Adrenaline spiked through my veins, and a crazy laugh tumbled out of me.

We'd gotten away. We've faced down criminals and survived—and I'd gotten what I'd come for.

Logan's car was parked right in front of mine. I fumbled for the key fob in my pocket as the guys gathered around their vehicle. A couple of the men from the bar had just made it out to the sidewalk, so we couldn't stick around for long, even if they wouldn't attack us quite as vehemently in full public view.

Still, Logan felt the need to turn toward me just as I yanked my car door open, his lips pulled back in a sneer. "Was that really worth it?"

I stared back at him, still high on the wildness of our victory, and held up Dad's box where they could all clearly see it.

"Yes," I said. "I'd say it was."

CHAPTER
TWENTY-FIVE

Madelyn

Somehow I wasn't surprised that the first thing Dexter did when we all ended up back in the Vigil office was ask for the box from me and then immediately start checking it over. Feeling wiped out from the stress—and, okay, the little bit of excitement—of the past couple of hours, I flopped into one of the chairs by the central table, watching him.

"Looking for secret compartments?" I asked.

"It is possible it's some kind of puzzle box, and your dad just never mentioned that specific aspect," he said. "I'm not seeing anything obvious, but if there's a hidden section, I'll find it eventually." He spoke mildly but with total confidence in his abilities. Kind of a welcome change from Logan a.k.a. Mr. Cocky.

Who'd propped himself against the computer desk and folded his arms over his chest, glowering at me with a scowl. I guessed it was only a matter of time before he decided to start berating me for my choice of actions with his words as well as his eyes. Never mind that I'd actually achieved the most important part of my goals in the end.

Never mind that I'd saved his *life*. Or maybe that was partly why he was pissed off—he didn't like that he couldn't claim I'd been completely inept.

I definitely wasn't expecting an apology for his cruel comments earlier today anytime soon.

Slade leaned against the table next to me and bumped his foot against one of the chair legs. "I knew you were kickass after the moves you showed off at the mechanic shop, but today was a totally new level. That'll teach us to underestimate you. And you found your dad's box too! You're going to put us out of a job."

I laughed a little roughly, knowing how close I'd been to potentially losing my own life. "Oh, I wouldn't go that far." But the praise felt good. It was nice to know someone here appreciated what I'd managed to accomplish, even if it hadn't been according to the Vigil's plans. "I just wanted to be an equal part in the investigation."

Logan snorted but still didn't speak. I bit back a snarky remark and focused on a question that'd started to bother me while I'd been driving back and the adrenaline rush of the fight had worn off. "There is something that doesn't make sense about this whole thing."

Dexter glanced up, still working over the box with

his deft fingers even without his full attention on it. "What's that?"

I frowned. "Why did those guys at the bar have the box at all? It seemed like the manager was checking it out, since it was on his desk. And I guess they were the ones who stole my car too?"

Slade shrugged. "They're part of a pretty large gang that's active in the city—we clashed with them over a different case last year, which must be how the one guy recognized Logan. Stealing stuff is par for the course with those types. They must have grabbed the car and then taken the box with them after they dropped it off in case it was valuable."

"But it wasn't," I pointed out. "It shouldn't have taken them long to figure that out, and then they'd have chucked it. It's been a week since my car was taken. And would a gang normally be all secretive about dropping off a car at a chop shop?"

Slade spread his hands. "Who knows? Criminals don't always think the ways the rest of us would find totally logical. Maybe one of the thieves knew his boss had a thing for Celtic knots."

"It's just hard to imagine it's something that random. It's weird that they picked my car to steal in the first place when they couldn't do more with it than sell it for parts, right?"

"It's not important," Logan snapped, finally speaking up. "You have it back. That's what you wanted, isn't it?"

I narrowed my eyes at him. "I think the reason it

was stolen is pretty important, because if they targeted me once over something like that, who knows whether they'll come after me in some other way again. Or if it had something to do with my dad somehow—"

Logan pushed off the desk and smacked his hands down on the edge of the table, outright glaring at me now. "There doesn't have to be a reason people do shitty things, Madelyn. It was probably just a bunch of punks being idiots to pass the time. Which we'd have found out on our own without you risking your life if you'd stuck to the plan instead of running straight into danger like you've got a death wish."

The anger I'd been suppressing flared to the surface. "I know I didn't handle it perfectly, and I'm sorry I had to drag you in to help me out of the blue. But it worked out to all our benefits in the end. If we'd stuck with *your* plan, we'd never have found the box at all or even known they had it. There's no way we'd have been sneaking into the office without being seen while the bar was open and there were employees and customers all over the place."

"If you had a problem with my plan, you should have talked to me about it and we'd have come up with a different one."

"Oh, sure, like you've listened to me so much before now."

His expression tightened. "I'd rather come up with a plan we can both agree on than have you pulling risky stunts that could get you killed."

For fuck's sake. "Right, and breaking into a

stranger's house wasn't risky? Shoving your way into a mechanic shop you know is involved in illegal dealings wasn't risky? It's not like we got attacked *there*—oh, wait, we did." My hand moved to the scabbed over scratch on my arm instinctively. "None of us knew the people in that bar were going to be that dangerous—or if you did, you didn't bother to fill me in. If you can take risks, so can I."

Logan let out a scoffing sound. "*I* know how to take care of myself."

"And so do I. Or did you miss the part where I saved my ass *and* yours in the end. You'd have gotten a bullet in the head if I hadn't jumped in there."

The thought of the gang woman having gotten off her shot, of Logan dying, sent a chill through me that doused some of my anger. But Logan kept going.

"We were only in that fight because you got yourself into a mess to begin with," he growled.

"And I'd have gotten out of the mess *without* a fight if you hadn't already been hassling gangsters all over town enough to get recognized," I shot back.

Logan leaned forward, his eyes flashing. "If you really think—"

Slade pushed between us, holding out his arms. "Whoa. I think that's enough arguing. We all made it out okay, and we got what we were searching for, so I think we should call that a win and stop making a pissing contest out of it." He aimed a hard look at Logan and then reached to take my hand. "Come on, Maddie. Let's take a little walk and give this guy time to cool off and figure out where he misplaced his gratitude."

Part of me didn't want to leave without finishing the argument, but a larger part realized it would probably never be finished. Logan was never going to give an inch of ground or admit that I'd been anything other than an idiot. Fine. I could use some space from him too.

I stood up and followed Slade out of the room without a backward glance. The door thumped shut behind us.

There wasn't much of anyone around to notice our exit. It was coming up on closing hours, the sunlight dwindling beyond the library windows. Only a few students remained up at the tables near the front, across from the checkout desk where a lone librarian remained on duty. The area at the back near the Vigil office and the rows of bookshelves was totally quiet.

Slade kept walking, guiding me between two of the shelving units where the sound of distant turning pages was even more dulled and there was no one around at all. He dropped his voice low. "Don't listen to him. He's just in a mood." He stroked his thumb over the back of my hand and offered a sly smile. "I happen to think you're one of the strongest and most capable women I've ever met—and that those features are incredibly sexy."

A blush singed my cheeks. I turned to face him, suddenly lost for words. Why was it that his flirty comments and the intensity in those dark eyes could leave me tongue-tied and flushed like a preteen with the world's biggest crush?

"Is that supposed to be a pick-up line?" I said, aiming for a teasing tone and not sure whether I landed it.

Slade chuckled. "Let's just call it the truth. But I can find other ways of complimenting you if you'd prefer a little more variety. Hay una fiesta en mi corazón y tú estás invitado."

My breath caught in my throat at the poetic lilt of the Spanish words. "What does that mean?"

He waggled his eyebrows. "Isn't the mystery part of the fun?"

I raised my own eyebrows right back at him. "You could have called me worse things than Logan did and I'd never know it."

Slade placed a hand over his chest as if I wounded him. "I would never call you anything insulting."

"And how can I be so sure about that?"

He shifted closer, forcing me to lean against the books behind me. His hand reached past me to rest against the shelf next to my arm while he pinned me with his gaze. My lower belly pulsed at his proximity, the scent of cinnamon reaching my nose from his breath.

His voice was a soft murmur now. "I might say that you're deslumbrante or absolutely impresionante, but I would never call you something that didn't fit."

My whole body was flushed now. "What do those words mean?"

He leaned forward, his lips a mere centimeter from mine. "I'm saying that you're breathtakingly beautiful, Piccolina. You're a masterpiece. I want to worship and appreciate you. I want you to forget about Logan for a little while and see how much you're worth."

I couldn't think of a time in the past few weeks when Logan had been farther from my mind. It was just Slade and me, standing face to face with a chemistry I couldn't deny. I didn't need or want to think about Logan. Only Slade. Why the hell shouldn't I pursue what we both obviously wanted?

I closed the last short distance between us and pressed my lips into Slade's with an intensity that he matched immediately. As he pressed the entirety of his body against mine, pinning me against the shelves, I wrapped one arm around his neck. He captured my mouth completely, every movement of his lips stealing more of my breath, until I felt as if I were drowning in him in the best possible way.

Slade smiled into the kiss, running his tongue over the tips of my teeth. He tightened his grip in the back of my shirt and ran his other hand slowly up and down my thigh. Sparks spread across my skin, and a little gasp escaped my mouth.

"The sounds you make are delectable," he whispered, and trailed his lips down my throat. His path of kisses seared across my neck and over my shoulder to the neckline of my shirt. I arched into him automatically, an ache of need pulsing between my legs.

It'd been a long time since I'd hooked up with

anyone—a long time since I'd wanted to this much. I had the urge to drag him straight back to my dorm room, but I couldn't quite bring myself to push him away in order to do that. The magic he was working with his mouth on my skin felt way too good.

He followed my shirt's neckline until his lips grazed my cleavage before claiming my mouth again with a heated passion that had my toes curling. His hands skimmed down my sides from my chest to my hips and then back up, dipping beneath the fabric of my shirt. The swipe of his thumbs over my belly provoked another soft noise from my throat.

My hips swayed toward him of their own accord and brushed against the bulge behind his slacks. My heart skipped a beat knowing how turned on he was by our collision, my panties dampening even more than they already had before. Then his hands closed over my breasts, and I had to swallow a whimper.

He worked over my curves with assured skill, tweaking my nipples until I was trembling with the jolts of bliss. My eyes slid closed, my lower lip clamped between my teeth as I struggled to hold back my sounds of encouragement. Then he dipped his fingers right beneath the cups of my bra to fondle me skin to skin, and an audible breath shuddered out of me.

"Just like that," Slade murmured, sounding a little hoarse, as if the gesture had affected him as much as it had me. As he kept caressing me with one hand, he eased the other down between us to the waistband of my pants. "Oh, Piccolina."

Everything about this—his skillful touch, the cinnamon flavor of his mouth as it devoured me whole, the sound of his voice to my ears—felt like an erotic fantasy that I'd never dared to consciously consider. The sensations swept through me, tearing me away from my physical reality and placing me only in his arms.

I quivered as his hand lowered inside my pants, sliding over my panties and rubbing a finger along the most sensitive part of me. The way his fingers worked, there might as well have been no barrier between us at all. He massaged my breast and swept his tongue across my bottom lip in tandem, and oh God, I didn't want this to end. All I wanted was to be consumed by Slade every way he would offer.

A distant thud from the other side of the library jarred me out of my blissful daze. My gaze darted to the end of the shelving unit, with a hitch of my pulse as I thought about how public this encounter was.

"Someone might see us," I murmured.

Slade gave me one of his sly grins, his eyes gleaming eagerly. He gripped my hips and spun me around so that I faced the shelves, my breasts pressing into the edge of one while I looked across the library through the narrow gap over the tops of the books. I could see one of the students standing up as she sorted through the books she'd brought to her table, another walking over to the checkout desk.

Slade traced his fingers over my thigh and delved beneath my pants again. "This makes it more fun," he said by my ear. "They have no idea what we're getting up to. But if you want to stop, just say the word."

Did I? My head was spinning with uncertainty and pleasure. The tip of his finger flicked over my clit, and I jerked in his arms with a gasp I couldn't hold back.

It felt so fucking good. And I was tired of trying to do the right thing, of trying to play by other people's rules. What we were doing wouldn't hurt anyone, and I needed everything Slade was giving me. I needed him.

I ground my ass against his erection in unspoken invitation. Slade hummed happily and tucked his hand right between my legs. "Good girl."

That comment alone had me melting in his arms, panting each of my breaths. As his hand moved back down to where I knew I'd entirely liquified, I couldn't stop the way my body jerked and writhed. Slade didn't seem to mind. He only held me there, pressing heated kisses into the side of my throat.

"You're so wet for me," he muttered into my ear. I bucked into his hand, and he began thrusting that damn finger right inside me. The sounds coming from my mouth were difficult to hold at bay, and one tumbled from my lips before I could stop it.

Slade nipped my earlobe. "Don't be too loud. We wouldn't want to get caught."

I could only nod, though I knew how hard it'd be to stay quiet if he kept up what he was doing to me right now. His fingers moved in lazy circles over the folds of my pussy, catching on that one desired spot long enough to have me stiffening and leaning my head back into his shoulder before he thrust a second long finger into me.

I clenched my teeth to avoid making any noises as he pulsed his fingers inside me, filling me until I was throbbing for more. "How do you like me now?" he rasped into my ear, and I almost couldn't suppress the moan that rushed up my throat.

The sound of footsteps came from the direction of the tables, and I froze, Slade's fingers still working inside of me. The girl I'd seen at the one table was walking toward the rows of bookshelves.

My heart stuttered for reasons that had nothing to do with my gratification. What if she walked all the way back here? Would we be able to pull ourselves together in time to hide what we'd been doing?

Slade's rhythm slowed as he picked up on the sound too. I was torn between the desire to start rearranging my clothes now and the stark resistance to the idea of ending this encounter before we'd seen it through. I was right on the verge of reluctantly pulling away from him when the footsteps stopped.

The girl turned into an aisle about five rows down. I watched over the tops of the books in front of me, my breath in my throat. She appeared to scan the titles she was facing and then grasped one of the books. Then, mercifully, she turned and walked back to the tables.

Slade let out a relieved chuckle and started stroking me again. "I think that's our sign that we shouldn't dawdle any longer while tempting fate," he said. "I don't want to finish this without you *fully* satisfied."

Before I could consider what he meant, he released my pussy just long enough to yank my pants and panties down to my knees. I bit back a gasp as he caressed my bare cheeks. "Ah, what an ass, Piccolina."

He gave one cheek a light slap with his open palm —surprising me and sending an unexpected jolt of pleasure through me. My back arched, pushing myself toward him instinctively, and I could hear the smirk in his voice. "Oh, you like that, do you? Who knew Maddie Silver was such a dirty girl behind that straight-laced exterior?"

He spanked me again, and my breath broke into panting. Then there was a rasp of a zipper as he opened his fly. With a crinkle of foil that was strangely reassuring despite the craziness of this whole encounter, he prepped himself. He must have had a condom in his pocket—did he do things like this a lot?

I didn't really care, not while he was doing it with me right now. This moment was all that mattered.

He rubbed his rigid shaft between my legs over my slick entrance, and the ache in my pussy intensified. "Don't make a noise," he reminded me in a mischievous tone, and then plunged all the way in.

He filled me so abruptly and completely that I thought I might explode just like that. A hissed swear word and a muffled groan burst from his own mouth. It took every ounce of my willpower to keep from releasing a moan as his fingers dug into my hips and he thrust into me again.

One of his hands left my hip to give me another soft

spank on my ass. I couldn't help it that time—the faintest of whimpers slipped from my lips.

"You like that?" he asked, picking up the rhythm of his thrusts as he massaged the spot he'd smacked. "I can give you all the attention you need. But if you don't stay quiet, I'm going to have to make you."

I knew it was meant to be a threat, but even as I tightened my grip on the bookshelf, I couldn't suppress the needy noises that were trickling out of me. With every stroke of his cock inside me, I was seeing stars. My body was outright shaking, my self-control fragmenting. Soon there was going to be nothing left in me but bliss.

"Then make me," I whispered.

Slade plunged into me faster at the comment. "That beautiful, filthy mouth is going to get you in trouble."

Despite my best efforts, a slightly louder moan seeped up my throat. True to his promise, Slade reached forward and pressed his hand against my mouth. His palm muffled my next cry, and something about the gesture made the moment even more thrilling. The pleasure surging inside me spiraled higher, stronger by the second.

"The next time we do this," Slade panted quietly, "we're going to go someplace where I can find out just how loud you can get."

I closed my eyes as he sped up even more, filling me even more deeply. He hit the perfect spot inside me, again and again, and then my climax roared through me.

As I shattered with my release, ecstasy sweeping

through me in a wave, Slade's hand clamped harder over my mouth to cover the little sounds of my release. His hips jerked, and his breath rasped as he followed me over.

I slumped against the shelves, coming down from my orgasm, and Slade released my mouth. I drew in a few ragged breaths and then glanced over my shoulder at him, taking in his exertion-flushed face and those sparkling eyes.

"Next time, I want to hear more from you too," I said.

A grin stretched across his face. "I do love it when you talk dirty, Maddie."

He was just sliding out of me when the door to the Vigil office swung open and Logan strode out right across from our aisle. He stalled in his tracks, staring straight at us.

CHAPTER
TWENTY-SIX

Madelyn

Logan froze for all of a second before he marched right into the aisle between the bookshelves, his eyes flashing with fury. As Slade hastily tucked himself back into his slacks, I fumbled to yank up my pants, a blush scorching my cheeks.

"What the fuck do the two of you think you're doing?" Logan spat out, stopping just a few feet from where we stood. He managed to keep his voice low despite its harshness, but his hands had clenched at his sides.

My first impulse was to say, "This isn't what it looks like," but it was exactly what it looked like. Why should I claim it wasn't? What Slade and I had decided to do had nothing to do with Logan. Nothing at all. He had no reason to be pissed off. If no part of his life was any of my business, then me hooking up with his friend sure as hell wasn't any of his.

So I raised my chin and glared right back at him. "I think it's pretty obvious."

"Really? Running off into a violent gang's bar wasn't enough—now you're fucking in public—in the goddamn university library? When did either of you get so stupid and reckless?"

"There wasn't anything stupid about it," I retorted, straining to keep my voice quiet too. The last thing we needed was the rest of the library's patrons noticing our argument. "We were enjoying ourselves. Sorry that's so hard for you to wrap your head around."

Logan threw his hands in the air. "Enjoying yourselves? What do you think would have happened to you if you'd gotten caught? You could have been expelled—they could have arrested you for indecent exposure." His furious whispers were becoming tauter with every sentence.

"We didn't get caught," I said. "No one came anywhere near us, and if they had, we'd have stopped. The only one who's having any problem with what we did is *you*."

Logan chuckled darkly and spun toward Slade, who'd stepped up beside me to slip his hand around my elbow. "And what were you trying to prove with this stunt, huh?"

Slade narrowed his eyes at him, tension humming through his stance. Logan might have been his best friend, but he wasn't any happier about being confronted like this than I was.

"It wasn't a stunt," he said, keeping his voice equally low. "We're into each other; she deserves someone who'll treat her right."

"Oh, and fucking her in the middle of the library is 'treating her right' now?"

Slade cocked his head, a little of his usual flippant attitude coming back into his pose. "Are you mad that we did something risky, or are you just angry because I hooked up with Maddie?"

"What the hell are you talking about?" Logan growled. "I don't give a shit what you do as long as you keep it in your pants in the middle of the goddamn university."

"Maddie's right," Slade replied. "We knew what we were doing. The only people around who had any chance of catching us by surprise were you and Dexter, and somehow I thought someone I consider a *friend* wouldn't be pissing all over me. So it seems to me like there's something more going on. Not that you have any right to be jealous after the way you've acted around her."

"I'm not *jealous*," Logan sputtered. "For fuck's sake—"

"You're something," I interrupted. "Maybe it's just an asshole, but at this point, I don't really care. You've spent the past two years—and most of the year before that too—pretending I don't even exist. What makes you think you have the right to question what I do now? It's got nothing to do with you."

An angry flush spread across Logan's face, but it took him a moment before he could continue his tirade. "You took my best friend and convinced him to risk his entire career for a quickie."

Slade made a noise in the back of his throat and offered a small smirk. "Actually, bro, I think I did most of the convincing. Don't downplay my excellent seductive skills here."

"I thought you were a little smarter than to let your dick steer the way," Logan snapped at him.

Slade just shrugged, a gesture I could tell pissed Logan off even more. "I'd say this decision was made with both heads, above and below, and it's not one I'd take back, no matter how much you rant about it."

Logan let out an inarticulate growl and yanked his attention to me again. "And you. What happened to Madelyn Silver, devoted student with all those ambitions? Since when did you become such a slut?"

He hurled the last vicious word at me with such vehemence that I reeled back a step as if he'd punched me.

Had he really called me that? Logan Brooks, my junior-high champion against bullies, a guy who'd probably slept with more girls than he could remember the names of, was throwing a slur at me as if my worth was based on who I had sex with?

Fuck that.

My own rage bubbled up inside me too fast for me

to hold it back. And maybe I didn't want to. Maybe it was time Logan got an equal dose of his own medicine. At least I could make my accusations without resorting to slander.

"Don't you *dare* call me horrible names and act like I'm some kind of evil seductress," I said, unable to stop my voice from rising regardless of the room around us. I jabbed my finger toward him. "At least I'm not going to fuck someone and then erase them from my life like they weren't worth more than a speck of dirt. At least I don't toss the people who care about me aside and then act like they're the problem when they call me on it."

Logan's jaw dropped. He looked like he was grappling for words, but I barreled onward before he could get anything out.

"You treated me like I was nothing for two years, and now that we've been forced to deal with each other, you've been insulting me and putting me down every chance you can get. Over what? The fact that we hooked up two years ago and you regret that? Guess what, you were there too. I didn't force you to do anything, and frankly, you seemed pretty fucking enthusiastic at the time. I gave you two years of space to get over whatever your issue with me is and you still act like I somehow ruined your life."

I was vaguely aware of Slade watching me with a mix of awe and shock, of my voice carrying through the library, but I couldn't bring myself to give a shit. It felt like too much of a relief to finally unleash all of this hurt and frustration.

"You talked like you were annoyed that I wanted anything from you, even just an explanation," I went on. "Like it's some awful thing that I have any feelings at all to do with you. But as soon as I'm focused on some other guy, you barge in and tear into me over that too? I obviously just can't win with you. Everything I do is wrong."

"Maddie," Slade said softly, and the tapping of footsteps reached my ears. I only pushed myself onward. I wasn't done yet.

I stepped forward, prodding my finger right against Logan's chest. "Guess what. You're getting your wish. We found everything I lost; you can shove me right back out of your life again. But you're not stopping me from seeing Slade, who I happen to like very much and who's been better to me in the past week than you've been in years. So you'll just have to get over that fact. Because the only person who's a problem right now is *you*, not me. And you're never going to convince me of the opposite again."

As my last words faded into the air, the librarian bustled into view, her eyes wide. "What on earth is going on over here?"

I dragged in a breath, jerking my gaze from Logan to her. "Nothing," I said. "Sorry for causing a commotion."

She tutted her tongue. "You can't be disturbing the other students, who are actually working here. If you need to have an argument, take it out of the building."

I dipped my head apologetically. "It's fine. I was leaving anyway. Again, I'm sorry."

The woman pursed her lips as I brushed past her, but I thought I caught a flicker of worry in her eyes. I had no idea how I looked after unloading all of my anger on Logan. I hurried to the front doors before she could ask if I was okay, before Logan could say anything that would only enrage me more.

As I pushed past the door, cool damp air washed over me. It didn't do much to douse the angry heat still pulsing through my body.

That'd been such an amazing moment with Slade. Risky, yes, but thrilling and sexy... I couldn't remember when I'd last felt that good. And now Logan had ruined it, spewed his resentment and hostility all over what should have been a giddy memory.

Why couldn't he let me have even one piece of happiness? How could he rant at me about being hung up on him and then attack me for moving on?

What had I done to make him hate me so much?

I gritted my teeth against the pang that came with that last thought. I hadn't done anything. The Logan I'd used to know had clearly changed into someone I barely recognized, someone I didn't even want to know. And that was fine.

We were done. None of that mattered. *Logan* didn't matter.

I strode on through the lengthening shadows toward my dorm building, looking forward to curling up on my bed and letting out a few final tears before I put all those churned-up emotions aside and focused on the future. Other than getting together with Slade again, I never needed to have anything to do with the Vigil guys again. I had my car back, and Dad's box—

My feet stalled in mid-step with a lurch of my heart.

The box. Dexter had been examining it in the Vigil office. I'd gotten so upset at Logan that I'd forgotten it when I'd stormed out of the library.

Shit.

I stood there for a moment, debating whether I really wanted to make the ten-minute trek across campus back to the law library immediately. Right when the other students still around would stare and Logan would glower at me and maybe have a few choice words.

But if I didn't go now, I had no idea what I'd face when I did go back. I just wanted this whole situation to be over with. Better to rip off that final bandaid than to draw things out.

Logan had gotten a little time to cool off after our argument. Maybe he'd even have headed out too, and I'd only have to deal with Slade and Dexter, who I had nothing against.

I could hope for that, but my body tensed in anticipation as I hurried along the campus paths. I would at least stay calm. No more yelling in the library. I couldn't regret what I'd said to him, but I didn't like pissing off the staff or disturbing the other students.

When I slipped back into the library, I found the main space empty. It was only fifteen minutes before closing now, and it looked like the remaining stragglers had cleared out. Even the check-out desk was abandoned, although I heard shuffling from the room behind it that suggested the librarian was sorting out some paperwork.

I hustled past, not wanting her to notice me and either send me off again or ask what was the matter. All I had to do was grab the box and get out of here again.

No one was standing around outside the Vigil office where I'd left Logan and Slade. I marched right up to the door and tried the handle. When it turned, I assumed someone was inside.

I tugged it open and found myself staring at a vacant room. No one sat at the table or the desk. They'd all cleared out.

But they'd left the door unlocked. That was strange. Maybe they'd been distracted by the argument?

Or by something else. My box was sitting on the table where Dexter must have left it. But it looked... odd. Because a tiny drawer, so shallow it couldn't have held anything much thicker than a business card, had been popped open on the side.

My pulse leapt. Dexter had discovered a secret compartment after all. It *had* been a puzzle box.

And there was something in the compartment. A slip of paper, looking like it was a corner torn off a larger sheet, with faded black pen ink scrawled across it.

I picked up the box and plucked the slip of paper out of the compartment. That was my dad's handwriting. I still had a few notes he'd written to me during my elementary school days, little messages of encouragement he'd randomly tuck inside my lunch box. I'd have recognized his arched letters anywhere.

The actual writing didn't make much sense to me. It was an address, but not one I was familiar with. No place I'd ever gone; not a street name I had any associations with.

Why had Dad written it down? Why had he felt the need to hide it away in this box in a super-secret drawer?

Did this have something to do with the reason the box had been stolen in the first place? Had those gangsters been looking for something like this inside it?

They hadn't found it... but the Vigil guys had. They'd left in a huge hurry afterward. *They* thought it was important—and they'd taken off to investigate without even letting me know.

Maybe they'd figured I wouldn't be interested in my current mood, but the knowledge still annoyed me. My jaw clenching, I tucked the paper into my pocket, hugged the box to my chest, and dashed out of the office. All my thoughts narrowed down to getting to my car so I could uncover this final mystery and how my dad factored into it before I lost my chance.

CHAPTER
TWENTY-SEVEN

Madelyn

Even after looking up the address on my phone's map app, I hadn't been prepared for exactly where I'd find myself when I drove out there. After getting off track a couple of times and having to stop briefly to re-orient myself, I ended up in an industrial neighborhood, cruising past old brick factories and warehouses.

Some of them were still in use—I saw smoke rising from one smokestack against the darkening sky and a delivery truck pulling out of a lot beside another—but others were obviously derelict. Broken windows gaped at me with jagged glass; others were boarded with plywood. For a couple of minutes before I arrived at the exact spot Dad had noted, there was no movement on the streets around me, no sound but the growl of my car's engine.

The fact that Dad had made special notice of a building out here made even less sense to me now. Maybe it'd had something to do with a medical research project—a public health and safety issue? But I couldn't imagine why he'd need to keep that secret. All of his work involved coordinating with other researchers and often hospital or government staff as well.

But if this didn't have anything to do with his work, what *could* it be about? Nothing about this situation fit what I'd known about my dad. Mom had certainly never hinted that there'd been anything mysterious about him or any more to him in general than I'd have noticed as a kid.

Was this something he'd hidden even from her?

As I squinted at the address numbers on the buildings, apprehension crawled over my skin. Did I really want to know what was going on here? Whatever it was, it'd ended twelve years ago when Dad had died, if not before. He *was* dead. Nothing he'd done could matter all that much, could it?

But whatever it was, the Vigil guys were already investigating it. I couldn't let *them* know more about my own father than I did. And Dad had been a guiding force for so much of my life…

If I didn't find out what was significant about the address, it was going to niggle at me forever. The truth couldn't be worse than the most horrible things I could imagine.

When I spotted Logan's car parked on the street up ahead, my resolve strengthened. They were still here. I could join up with them and insist that they shared whatever they'd already discovered. That Slade and Dexter did, anyway. I had no interest in saying anything else to Logan.

The building that matched the address from the box was one of the abandoned warehouses. Ratty cardboard had been taped over the lower windows; the hinges on the front door were rusty. It hung ajar, but there was no way of telling whether it'd been left that way or if Dexter had opened it with his lock-picking skills.

The worn red bricks held no sign indicating what company the building belonged to or anything else about it. It was totally blank.

A shiver crawled over my skin, but the guys were already inside. And the place obviously wasn't being used anymore. What could be so bad in there? We'd be lucky if we came across anything at all that might have involved my dad more than a decade ago.

I got out of the car and walked up to the warehouse. The hinges creaked as I pulled the door just wide enough to slip inside.

There was no entryway. I stepped straight into a large, dim room with a ceiling that stretched at least two floors high. A stale, slightly sour scent tickled my nose. Other than a few dusty shipping crates stacked off to the side, looking as if no one had touched them in years, the room held nothing but a cracked concrete floor, marked with smudges and stains where equipment had once stood, and silence.

Only silence for a moment. Faint voices carried

from the other side of the room. There were a few doorways set in the wall there between uncovered windows that let in a little of the dwindling daylight through the grime. I hurried over, wincing inwardly at the scrape of my sneakers against the gritty floor despite my efforts at placing them quietly.

If the guys had found something, I didn't want to give them the chance to hide it from me. Who knew what Logan would decide was too risky for me to be a part of now?

I followed the voices to the doorway that was the farthest to the right. I started to distinguish words. It sounded like Slade was swearing.

"We'll figure it out," Logan muttered.

They'd figure out *what*? I marched up to the doorway—and jerked to a halt at the sight that met my eyes.

The three guys were crouched at the far end of a much smaller room that looked as if it might have been some kind of office at one point. The cardboard had fallen off the window there too, allowing the thin evening light to stream over the scene. A storage cabinet stood against one wall, and a long narrow desk filled most of the space near the guys.

But I only registered those sparse details in the first instant when I glanced through the room. What arrested me was the body lying on the floor at the Vigil guys' feet.

It was a man—I couldn't make out much more about him in the dimness from ten feet away. Other than the stream of stark red flowing down his pale shirt from the spot where a knife had been stabbed right into his chest in the area of his heart.

A knife Logan was in the middle of reaching for, his sleeve streaked with the same scarlet blood.

I gasped, and the guys whirled around. It wasn't just his sleeve—Logan had blood splashed all over the front of his shirt. More blood was pooling beneath the corpse from what was obviously an incredibly fresh wound.

A chill flooded my entire being. Oh, God. Logan had *killed* that man.

And the three of them had been standing around deciding what to do with the body.

All of the guys' expressions had frozen in startled, horrified masks. Slade managed to find his voice first, scrambling upright with a slight wobble of his normally steady prosthetic leg that revealed just how off-balance he was. "Maddie—it's not what it looks like. I swear—"

How could it not be what it looked like? My stepbrother wasn't just an asshole. He was a murderer.

One panicked thought blared through my mind: I had to get out of here.

I propelled myself backward and spun around in the same movement, intending to race back to my car. But I slammed straight into the hulking form of a man I hadn't heard coming up behind me.

The massive stranger clamped his hands around my arms with a menacing snarl. "You're not going anywhere."

ABOUT THE AUTHORS

Eva Chance is a pen name for contemporary romance written by Amazon top 100 bestselling author Eva Chase. If you love gritty romance, dominant men, and fierce women who never have to choose, look no further.

Eva lives in Canada with her family. She loves stories both swoony and supernatural, and strong women and the men who appreciate them.

Connect with Eva online:
www.evachase.com
eva@evachase.com

Harlow King is a long-time fan of all things dark, edgy, and steamy. She can't wait to share her contemporary reverse harem stories.